T0346831

THE
INSTRUCTIVE and ENTERTAINING

FABLES

OF

PILPAY,

AN

Ancient *Indian* PHILOSOPHER

Containing a NUMBER of Excellent

RULES

For the CONDUCT of Persons of all AGES,
and in all STATIONS: Under several HEADS.

THE FIFTH EDITION,
Corrected, Improved, and Enlarged; and Adorned
with near Seventy CUTS neatly Engraved.

---

*Fable is not only the surest way of giving Counsel, but that which
pleases the most universally.* ADDISON.
*After the Sacred Writings, there is no Work to which the World in
general has paid so great an Esteem as the Fables of* Pilpay—*They
have been translated into almost all the known Languages.*
Dict. de MORRERI.

---

*DARF PUBLISHERS LTD:
LONDON
1987*

NEW IMPRESSION 1987

ISBN 1 85077 144 8

Printed and bound in Great Britain by
A. WHEATON & Co. Ltd., Exeter, Devon.

PREFACE.

It may not be improper to inform the Reader, that the Fables contained in this Treatise, though but little known in our Part of the World, are in many of the Eastern Nations, at this time, universally read, and esteemed an inestimable Treasure of Knowledge and Instruction; and that the Author is so highly admired there, that *Pilpay*, for so he was called, is with them a Name as much honoured as that of *Æsop* in many other Nations.

This *Pilpay*, was an *Indian* Philosopher, a Man of high Rank in that Nation, and of great Renown for his Wisdom throughout all the East; he was of that Sect which the Natives of those Places call *Bramins*, a Name like that of the *Magi* or *Druids* of some other Nations, expressing, that those who are honoured with it are Persons of extraordinary Learning and Wisdom.

This renown'd Philosopher composed this little Work when he governed a Part of *Indoston*, under the Sovereignty of the most potent Monarch *Dabschelim*. *Pilpay* has displayed all his Wisdom in this little Piece; and according to the custom of the Eastern People, who never teach but in Parables, he here lays before all the Kings and Princes the best and wisest Methods of governing their Subjects, couched under the Disguise of Histories of Things which happened among Birds and Beasts, as well as those of his own Species.

Dabschelim for a long time kept this Work as a great Secret, and left it as a most sacred Treasure to his Successors, among whom it remained unknown to all the World beside, till the Reign of *Nouschirvan* King of *Persia*.

This Prince, who was a Man of great Wisdom and Curiosity, having heard much talk of the Book, sent his principal Physician, a Man in whose Fidelity and Address he could confide, to the *Indies*, on purpose to procure a Copy of it. The Physician discharged himself of his Trust, to the great Satisfaction of his Master, brought him the Books into *Persia*; and being a Person who perfectly understood the Indian Language, translated the Fables into the ancient *Persian* Tongue; and this was the first public Edition of this most excellent work.

Many Ages after this, the *Arabians,* after they had conquered the finest Provinces of the East, and began to polish the Rudeness of their Manners with the Ornaments of Learning, not only endeavoured to render their Language copious and delightful, but invited into their Country the most wise and learned Persons of all the Nations of the World; to whom they gave great Rewards for translating the most remarkable Books of every Country. And at this time *Aboul Hassan Abdalla Almansor* translated these Fables out of the *Persian* into *Arabic,* by order of *Abou-Giafor Almansar,* the *Abassid.*

This Translation was soon after attended by another into the *Persian,* by Command of *Nasreh Ben Ahmad.* And after all these, *Nasrallah, Ben Mahoumed, Ben Abdelhamed,* translated them also into the same Language. This last Translation is greatly superior to all the others, and is the very Edition now used throughout a great Part of the East, and from this (a Copy of which was some Years ago brought over by a Gentleman who had travelled over those Countries) the Translation we present the Reader with, was originally made. Those who are not ignorant of the various Translations of *Aristotle, Euclid,* and *Ptolemy,* into *Greek, Syriac, Arabic,* and other Languages, will not be surprized at the several Translations of this Book: It is a Thing which frequently happens to good and useful Books; and they will esteem this the more for it, since frequent Translations are the most certain Evidences of the Excellency of a Work. Nor should we omit to mention in this Place, that the learned *Bezourg Ommid,* in his Answers to *Chosrou* upon the most intricate Doubts and puzling Questions, while he makes use of these Fables, gives a lasting Proof of their Value and general Utility.

There is no need of going far to prove the great Use of this way of conveying Instruction by Fables. What must give an everlasting and alone sufficient Sanction and Honour to it is, that it was the Practice observed by the Saviour of the World among those to whom he spoke: To whom, as the gospel tells us, he explained himself particularly in Parables. And if we have Occasion to seek farther back than that, the Fable or Parable in the sacred Scriptures of the *Old Testament,* of the Trees chusing themselves a King, as it is recited in the *Second Book of* Kings, is a sufficient Testimony of the Honour done to this allegorical way of Writing. And since that time the *Jews* have so continued this manner of expressing their Sense, and unfolding their Doctrines, and the Esteem they had it in cannot be concealed from those who have perused their Writings. In the *Talmud, Bereschit, Rabba, Zohar,* &c. they make the Waters, Mountains, Trees, and Letters themselves to speak.

The rest of the Orientals have in this also followed the Example of the *Hebrews*; the *Indians* and our Author; and the Parable of *Sandhaber* are still extant in the *Hebrew*. The *Egyptians* and *Nubians* have their *Lochman,* the most ancient of all the rest, since *Mirkhond* in his first Volume makes him cotemporary with *David.* And the *Arabians* also have a large Book of Fables, which is in great Reputation among them; and the author of which is highly applauded by their false Prophet.

The Esteem for this manner of writing became afterwards so great in the World, that the *Greeks* became Imitators of the *Eastern* Nations in it. And this cannot be doubted by any, since the *Greeks* themselves acknowledge that they derived this sort of Learning from *Æsop,* who was an Oriental. Among the modern Writers, the excellent Mr *Addison* observes, 'That Fables were the first Pieces of Wit that made their Appearance in the World, and have been still highly valued, not only in times of the greatest Simplicity, but among the most polite Ages of Mankind.' And in other Places; 'That Allegories, when well chosen, are like so many Tracks of Light in a Discourse that make every thing about them clear and beautiful.'

An even speaks with Honour of that kind of Writing, wherein the Poet quite loses Sight of Nature, and entertains his Readers Imagination with Characters and Actions of such Persons as have no Existence but what the author bestows upon them. Let this justify our excellent author in his Fable of the Angel, Ruler of the Sea, and whatever other are his bolder Passages.

That Fable in general has been the most ancient of all ways of instructing, is unquestionable; and it has always been so well received, that to condemn it, is deaclaring against the common Sense of Mankind. Young People, as another very excellent author observes, are exceeding fond of Fables; and it is good to take advantage of that Fondness for honest Purposes.

And the Fables of this author have this particular Advantage, that thro' the whole Book one is made the Introduction to Another, in such manner, that it is not easy, when once entered on reading it, to leave off before the End of a Chapter. This has been by some objected to, as a Fault in the Work, but I cannot help thinking that it is one of its greatest Beauties. The manner of making one Story introduce another, has ever been admired as one of the greatest Beauties of *Ovid's Metamorphoses,* and is plainly here of greater Use, as in the Works of this kind of other Authors, when a Person has read one Fable, which is a detached Piece, and has no Dependance on the rest, he has done, and his Mind is satisfied; whereas here when a young Person has read one Fable, the Author has so contrived it, that his Curiosity is excited to go thro' another, and so on to the End of that Chapter; in which also by the excellent Contrivance of the Author, the same set of Morals are inculcated in a Variety of beautiful Relations.

But we shall now leave the Reader to make his own Reflections, observing only this in general, That one of the Reasons which obliged the Eastern People to make use of Fables in their Instructions and Admonitions was, That the Eastern Monarchies being for the most part absolute, their Subjects were always restrained from Freedom of Speech. the Result of which was, that being an ingenious People, they found out this way, whereby they might be able, without exposing their Lives to imminent Danger, to inform and advise their Princes of what most nearly concerned the Welfare both of themselves and their Subjects, and instruct them, without giving Offence, in the Paths of Virtue, Honour and true Glory.

C O N T E N T S

G E N E R A L H E A D S.

———————✰✰✰✰✰———————

CONTENTS.

THE

FABLES

OF

PILPAY

INTRODUCTION

Towards the Eastern Confines of *China* there once reigned a Monarch, whose Renown, as well for Arms as Wisdom and virtue, spread far and near, through all the Countries of the East, and made him the Admiration of all that Part of the World. The greatest Princes of the East were subject to his Dominion, and Admirers of his Virtues. He was attended like *Cohadan,* and lodged like *Poashti**; potent as *Alexander,* and armed like *Darius.* His Council was composed of Persons of Integrity and Learning; his Riches were immense, his Armies numerous, and himself both valiant and just. Rebels felt his Anger, and his Soldiers imitated his Valour; his Justice humbled the Pride of Tyrants, while his Goodness succoured the Miserable. In a Word, under the Empire of *Humayon-Fal,* for so this virtuous Prince was called, the People were happy because every where

---

* *Cohadan* and *Poashti* were two Eastern Princes famous for their Conquests and Magnificence through all that Part of the World.

throughout his vast Dominions the most strict Search was made after the Wicked, and care taken to punish them as Enemies to the public Tranquillity.

Justice ought to be the Rule of every Prince's Actions, who desires his Kingdom and his Throne should be established like the Residence of the Supreme; and whatever Monarch omits to administer Punishments to Vice, and Rewards to Virtue, let him be assured his Dominions will not be long secure from Ruin.

Good Kings generally make good Servants, and so it happened to this excellent Monarch; for he had a Vizir, or Prime Minister, who loved the People like a real Father; he was merciful and compassionate; and his Counsels, like Tapers, gave light into the most hidden Secrets. His Name was *Gnogestebrai*, that is to say, successful Counsel, and very properly was he so called, since by his Understanding he had rendered the Kingdom happy. The King never undertook any Enterprize without first consulting him. He did everything by his Advice, for he found that without it nothing prospered.

It happened that once as the Monarch attended by his Vizir had been hunting, after the Pleasure and Sport of their Exercise were over, the King was for returning to his Palace: But the Heat of the Sun was so violently scorching, that he told the Vizir, he was not able to endure it. To which the Vizir answered, That, if it were his Majesty's Pleasure, he might go to the Foot of a certain neighbouring Mountain, where he would be sure of a cool Shade, and the refreshing Breezes of the Wind; and there they might pleasantly spend the Heat of the Day. The King followed his Advice; and in a little time they got to the Place, where the Coolness, caused by the Shade of several Trees that Nature seemed to have taken delight to plant by the Sides of a Number of winding Brooks and Fountains, make them forget the Heat which they had endured upon the open Road. The King, finding the Covert very delightful, sat down upon the Grass, and falling into a Contemplation of the Works of the great Creator of all Things, admired the inimitable Painting of the Flowers, and other Productions of Nature, that offered themselves to his Sight.

As he was with this most laudable View looking about him, he spied at some little Distance the Trunk of a Tree, which the Rottenness of the Wood declared to be decayed, and very old, in which there was a Swarm of Bees that were making Honey. Upon this, having never seen an Object of this Kind before, he could not avoid asking the Vizir, what those little Creatures were? Most Sovereign Monarch, replied that Minister, those little Creatures are very beneficial, and of a thousand Uses in Society; and are in the highest Degree remarkable for the Order of their Government. They have a King among them, who is bigger than the rest, and whom they all obey; he resides in a little square Apartment, and has his Vizirs, his Porters, his Serjeants, and his Guards; the Industry of these, and all his other Officers, and People in general, is such, that they frame every one for themselves a little six-cornered Chamber of Wax, the Angles of which differ not at all in Shape or Dimensions, but are so exactly made to answer one another, that the most expert Geometrician could not range them with more Regularity. These little Chambers finished, the Vizir takes of them an Oath of Fidelity, that they are never to defile themselves. According to which Promise, they never light but upon the Branches of Rose-bushes or odoriferous Flowers; so that their Food, which is aerial, and of the Quintessence of Flowers, is digested in a little time, and changed into a Substance of a sweet and pleasing Taste. When they return home the porters smell to them and if they have no ill Scent about them they are permitted to enter; but if they have any ungrateful Smell they kill them: Or if they negligently suffer any one that has an ill Scent to enter, and the King happens to smell it, he sends for the Porters, and puts them and the Offender to death at the same time. If any strange Fly endeavours to enter this Community, the Porters oppose him; and, if he seeks to come in by Violence, he is put to death. Historians also report to us, *Great Emperor!* that *Poashti* learnt to build his Palace, to have Vizirs, Porters, Guards, and Officers, from these little Creatures.

When the King had heard the Vizir thus discourse, he went near the Tree, stood still to behold the little Animals at Work, and after he had well considered them, declared aloud his Admiration to see a Society of Insects so well governed. His Vizir beholding his wrapt up in Astonishment, addressed himself to him in this manner: Sir, said he, all this good Order depends only upon the good Counsel and prudent Conduct of wise and able Ministers, well affected to their Prince, and Lovers of the public Peace;

there are the Persons that always preserve an Empire in a flourishing Condition: And whenever these Things are mentioned: we ought to remember the strongest Instance of this Maxim ever known, which was in the Conduct of the Great *Dabschelim*, who wholly entrusted the Government of his Kingdoms to the good Counsels of that Miracle of Wisdom, the *Bramin Pilpay*; insomuch, that, by the Guidance of that Minister, he reign'd in Peace and the greatest Prosperity, and earthly Happiness, while he lived, and dying left to his Posterity a Name for ever to be remembered with Esteem and Honour.

When the King heard him pronounce the Names of *Dabschelim* and *Pilpay*, he felt in himself the Motions of a more than ordinary Joy. I have, said he to the Vizir, for a long time most earnestly desired to hear the Story of that *Bramin's* Government, but never yet could meet with an Opportunity to satisfy myself, nor ever imagined that you knew their History. I am now more happy than I could expect, and desire you will immediately relate to me the Story, that my Kingdom may be established in Happiness by the Maxims of that venerable Philosopher. On this Command of the Monarch, the Vizir thus entered on the History.

———————— ⋆☆☆☆⋆ ————————

C H A P. I.

F O R T U N E *favours the* B O L D.

The Story of DABSCHELIM *and* PILPAY.

ON the Banks of *Indus,* towards the Sea-Coast, and over a vast Extent of Country thereabouts, there reign'd a Prince, whose Ministers (Persons of Justice, Wisdom, and Understanding) by their Counsels rendered the Subjects happy, and always successfully brought to pass the just Designs of the Sovereign. This excellent Prince was an Enemy to Oppression; nor could the Wicked ever gain their Ends in his Dominions. He was called *Dabschelim* (a Name most proper for such a Prince, as signifying in their Language, a *Great King.*) His Puissance was such, that he undertook none but extraordinary Enterprizes, and those always just, and on honest and honourable Grounds: To relieve the Distressed, or punish the proud Oppressor, were the only Occasions of his entering on War. His Army was composed of ten thousand Elephants, valiant and experienced Soldiers he had about him in great Numbers, and his Treasures were kept full to support them. This rendered him formidable to his Enemies, and procured the Repose of his People; of whom he took a particular Care, hearing their Complaints and Differences, composing their Quarrels, and making himself the Arbitrator of their Disputes, without any Respect to his Greatness or superior Rank. He never forsook the Interests of his People; but referred their Affairs, when of too long and intricate a Nature to come under his own Cognizance, to the Debates and Decisions of Men of Justice and Equity. When he had taken this good Order for the Government of his Dominions, he lived in Tranquility, and spent his Days with Happiness and Content. It happened that this wise and glorious Monarch, one Day, when he had been for a long

Time entertained with divers Discourses upon the several Sciences, and the Use they, and the Principles of Equity and Honour, must be of in the well-governing a People, laid himself down upon his Bed to give some Relaxation to his Mind; which he had no sooner done, but he saw in a Dream, a Figure full of Light and Majesty, which approaching toward him with a Look of Benevolence, and the highest Favour, spoke in the following Manner: *You have done this Day as a good Prince ought to do, and you shall be rewarded for it. To-morrow by break of Day get on Horseback, and ride toward the East, where you shall find an inestimable Treasure, by the means of which you shall, as you deserve, exceed in Glory and Honour all other Men.* Immediately the Figure disappeared, and *Dabschelim*, awaking with a Heart full of Joy and Gratitude, mounted one of his best Horses, and rode directly Eastward. He passed in his Way through several inhabited Places, but at length arrived in a Desart, where viewing the Country, and casting his Eyes on every Side, to discover his expected Happiness, he perceived, at a little Distance before him, a Mountain that reached above the Clouds, at the Foot of which he spied a Cave, obscure, dark, and black within as the Hearts of wicked Men. Without it he saw sitting a Man, whose whole Aspect sufficiently shewed the Austerity of his Life. The King had a great Desire to ride up to him, when the old Man, understanding his Intention, came forward; and breaking Silence, addressed himself to the Monarch in these Words: "Sir, said he, though my small Cottage be nothing like to your magnificent Palace, yet it is an ancient Custom for Kings, out of their Goodness, to come and visit the Poor. The Looks of great Men, cast down upon the mean, augment their own Grandeur. I joy to see the greatest and the wisest Monarch in the East not forget this ancient Custom. And, O! supreme and magnificent Prince, let it not raise a Blush in thee to cast thy Royal Looks on my low Estate, when thou rememberest that *Solomon*, in the midst of all his Glory and Magnificence, vouchsafed to cast his Eyes upon the little Ants."

Dabschelim was pleased with the old Man's Civility, and alighted from his Horse to discourse with him. After he had talked to him of diverse Things, and was going to take his leave, the venerable Sage surprized him with the following Words. "Sir, said he, 'tis not for a poor Man, as I am, to offer any Refreshment to so great a Prince as you; but permit me to tell you that I have a Present, if your Majesty pleases to accept it, which has descended to me from Father to Son, and which is appointed for you: It is a Treasure which I have here by me, though I know not myself exactly the Place where it now lies; but if your Majesty thinks it worth your Acceptance, command your Servants to seek for it." *Dabschelim,* hearing these Words, recounted his Dream to the good old Man, who rejoiced extremely to find that his Intentions in bestowing his Treasure were conformable to the Will of the supreme Power, by whom he was intrusted with it.

The King now commanded his Servants to search for the Treasure round about the Cave; in a little time they discovered it, and brought before the King a vast Number of Chests and Coffers full of Gold, Silver, and Jewels. Among the rest, there was one Chest of a smaller Size than the others, which was bound about with several Bars of Iron, and fastened with a Multitude of Padlocks, the Keys of which were not to be found notwithstanding all the Care and Diligence that were used to seek them. This highly increased the Monarch's Curiosity. "There must be something, said he, in this little Casket much more precious than Jewels, since it is so strongly and carefully barred and locked." A Smith was now procured, and the Casket being broken open, there was found within it another small Trunk of Gold, set all over with precious Stones, and within that yet another lesser Box; this the King ordered to be delivered into his own Hands. When this little Box was opened, he found therein a Piece of white Sattin, upon which were written some Lines in the *Syriac* Language. *Dabschelim* was astonished at the Accident, and in great Perplexity to know what the Words might signify. Some said, it was the Will of the Owner of the Treasure; and others, that it was a *Talisman,* or some Charm for the Preservation of it. After every one had delivered his Opinion, 'twas the King's Pleasure that Enquiry should be made for some Person who was able to interpret the Meaning of the Lines; and after long Search, a Person was found who perfectly understood all the Oriental Languages, who, when he had looked over it, said to the King, "Sir, this Writing is to a Prince, indeed, an inestimable Treasure; it contains the Rules, Admonitions and Instructions of a great King, for the well-governing a

People; and how nearly it particularly concerns yourself, Oh King! permit me to shew, by reading to you what it contains." The King bidding him read aloud, he then began as follows:

The Writing of the great King Houschenk, *left with his Treasures.*

I King *Houschenk,* have disposed of this Treasure for the Use of the great King *Dabschelim,* understanding, by a visionary Revelation, him to be the Person for whom it is designed; and among the precious Stones I have concealed this my last Will and Testament, by way of Instruction to him, to let him know that it is not for Men of Reason and Understanding to be dazzled with the Lustre of glittering Treasures. Riches are but borrowed Conveniences, and are to be repaid to our Successors. The Pleasures of this World are charming, but they are not eternal. This Testament is a Thing of much more real Use that all these Treasures: It is an Abridgment of the good rules proper to regulate the Conduct of Kings; and he must be a wise Prince who regulates his Conduct by these Instructions; which are in Number fourteen.

I. *That he never discard his domestic Servants at the Solicitation of other Persons.* For he that is near the Person of a King, will never want some who will be envious and jealous of his Happiness; and when they see that the King has any Affection for him, will not cease, by a thousand Calumnies, if it can be done, to render him odious to his Master.

II. *That he never suffer in his Presence Flatterers nor Railers;* for these People are always seeking Occasions of Disturbance. 'Tis better to exterminate such People from the Earth, than to let them be a Trouble to human Society.

III. *That he always preserve his Ministers and Grandees, if it be possible, in a right Understanding with one another;* to the End that they may unanimously labour for the Good and Welfare of the State.

IV. *That he never trust to the Submission of his Enemies.* The more Affection they testify, and the louder Protestations they make of their Services, the more Artifices and Villanies are to be mistrusted in them. *There is no relying upon the Friendship of an Enemy;* he is to be shunned when he approaches with the Countenance of a Friend, as the Syren who puts on Charms but with an Intent to destroy.

V. *When a Man has once acquired what he has diligently sought after, let him preserve it carefully; for we have not every Day the same Opportunity to gain what we desire.* And when we have not preserved what we have once acquired, we have nothing left us but the Vexation of having lost it. *We cannot fetch the Arrow back which we have once let fly, though we should eat our Fingers for Madness.*

VI. *That we never ought to be too hasty in Business;* but on the other Side, before we put any Enterprize into Execution, it behoveth us to weigh and examine what we are going to do. Things done in haste, and with a precipitate Rashness, come frequently to a mischievous Conclusion. He repents in vain who cannot recall what he has done amiss.

VII. *That a Man never despise good Counsel and Prudence.* If there be a necessity for him to make Peace with his Enemies, in order to deliver himself out of their Hands, let him do it without Delay.

VIII. *To avoid the Company of Dissemblers, and never to hearken to their smooth Speeches;* for as in their Bosoms they carry nothing but the Plants of Enmity, they can never bring forth the Fruits of Friendship.

IX. *To be merciful.* Never let a Monarch inflict a Punishment on his Subjects or Servants for Faults committed through Infirmity: For a merciful Prince upon Earth is as an Angel in Heaven. We ought to consider the Weakness of Men, and in Charity and Goodness to conceal their Defects. Subjects have always committed Faults, and Kings have always pardoned them, when they have only committed the Faults which the common Frailties of human Nature have betrayed them into.

X. *Not to procure the Harm or Injury of any Person.* On the other hand, we ought to do our Neighbour all the Good we can. *If you do Good, Good will be done to you; but if you do Evil, the same will be measured back to you again.*

XI. *That a King seek not after any thing that may be below his Dignity, or a Subject what is contrary to his Genius or Nature.* There are many Persons who let alone their own Affairs, to intrude themselves into other People's Business, and at last do nothing at all. The Crow would needs learn to fly like the Partridge; it was a Way of flying which he could never attain; and in attempting to learn it, he forgot his own.

XII. *To be of a mild and affable Temper.* Mildness in Society is like Salt in our Food: As Salt seasons and gives a

Relish to all Meat, and other gives Content to every body. The Sword of Steel is not so sharp as the Sword of Mildness; it vanquishes even invincible Armies.

XIII.   *For a King to seek out faithful Ministers, and never to admit into his Service or Councils Knaves and Deceivers.* By wise and honest Ministers the Kingdom will be kept safe, and the King's Secrets will never be revealed.

XIV.   *Never to disturbed at the Accidents of the World.* A Man of Resolution and true Courage suffers all Adversities with a settled Fortitude, and relies upon the Providence of Heaven, while a Fool minds nothing but his Pastime and his Pleasure.

There are several Fables of excellent Instruction founded on every one of these Heads, which if the King will hear, he must go to the Mountain *Serandib,** which was the Mansion of our Fathers, and there all the Histories composed to illustrate and explain these Admonitions will be related to him, and every Question that can come into his Heart to ask, concerning the making his People happy, will be answered as from an Oracle of Heaven.

When the learned Man had done reading, *Dabchelim* caught him in his Arms, and eagerly embraced him; and having received back again the Piece of Sattin, which he took with the most profound Respect, he tied it about his Arm, saying at the same time, I was promised indeed a worldly Treasure, but beside I have found a Treasure of Secrets. Heaven has favoured me with Plenty of its Blessings, for which my grateful Soul now offers its most humble Adorations and Praises. Having said this, he ordered the Gold and Silver to be distributed to the Poor, and returned to his Palace, where all that Night he did nothing but ruminate upon the Journey which he was to make to *Serandib*.

The next Morning, by Sun-rise, *Dabschelim* sent for two of his principal Ministers, in whom he had a great Confidence: To these he discovered his Dream, and what had afterwards befallen him, and told them he had a most earnest Inclination to make a Journey to *Serandib*. I have for a long time, said he, taken this Course, to advise with my Council before I undertook any of my Enterprizes, and in this also I

---

* A vast Mountain, famous for the Residence of many learned Men of the East.

am willing to refer myself to your Judgments. And now I have told you my Intentions, and the Reason of them, I conjure you by your Honours, and the Esteem I have for you, to tell me what you think, as a Prince who knows his Duty to be the Care of his Subjects, I ought to do on this Occasion. The two Ministers desired the Remainder of the Day and the Night following, to consider the whole Matter, that they might not without due Deliberation give their Answer in a Thing of so high Concernment. *Dabschelim* granted their Request, and the next Day they came to wait upon the King; and every one being seated in their Places, so soon as the Monarch made them the Sign to speak, the Grand Vizir fell upon his Knees and thus began.

Sir, In my Opinion, this Journey is like to be more painful than profitable. Your Majesty is to consider, that the Person who undertakes long Journies renounces at the same time in Repose; add to this, your Majesty is not ignorant of the Dangers and Hazards to which the Roads are subject. 'Tis not for a Person of Discretion to change his Quiet and Ease for Labour and Disturbance. Permit me on this Occasion to call to your Majesty's Remembrance the Fable of the Pidgeon that would needs be a Traveller, and the Dangers which he met with.

F A B L E I.

The TRAVELLING PIDGEON.

THERE were once in a certain Part of your Majesty's
Dominions two Pidgeons, a Male and a Female, which had
been hatched from the same Brood of Eggs, and bred up
together afterwards in the same Nest, under the Roof of an
old Building, in which they lived together, in mutual
Content and perfect Happiness, safely sheltered from all
the Injuries of the Weather, and contented with a little
Water and a few Tares. *'Tis a Treasure to live in a Desart, when
we enjoy the Happiness of a Friend; and there is no Loss in quitting
for the sake of such a one, all other Company in the World.* But it
seems too often the peculiar Business of Destiny to separate
Friends. Of these Pidgeons the one was called the *Beloved*,
and the other the *Lover*. One Day the *Lover* having an eager
Desire to travel, imparted his Design to his Companion.
Must we always, said he, live confined to a Hole? No; be it
with you as you please, but for my part I am resolved to take
a Tour about the World. Travellers every Day meet with
new Things, and acquire Experience; and all the Great and
Learned among our Ancestors have told us, that Travelling

is the only Means to acquire Knowledge. *If the Sword be never unsheathed, it can never shew the Valour of the Person that wears it; and if the Pen takes not its Run through the Extent of a Page, it can never shew the Eloquence of the Author who uses it.* The Heavens, by reason of their perpetual Motion, exceed in Glory and Delight the Regions beneath them; and the dull brute Earth is the solid Place for all Creatures to tread upon, only because it is immoveable. If a Tree could remove itself from one Place to another, it would neither be afraid of the Saw or the Wedge, nor exposed to the ill Usage of the Wood-mongers.

All this is true, said the *Beloved*; but, my dear Companion, you know not, nor have you ever yet undergone the Fatigues of Travel, or do you understand what it is to live in foreign Countries; and believe me, Travelling is a Tree, the chiefest Fruit of which is Labour and Disquiet. If the Fatigues of travelling are very great, answered the *Lover*, they are abundantly rewarded with the Pleasure of seeing a thousand Rarities; and when People are once grown accustomed to Labour, they look upon it to be no Hardship.

Travelling, replied the *Beloved*, my dear Companion, is never delightful but when we travel in company of our Friends; for when we are at a far Distance from them, besides that we are exposed to the Injuries of the Weather, we are grieved to find ourselves separated from what we love: Therefore take, my Dearest, the Advice which my Tenderness suggests to you: Never leave the Place where you live at Ease, nor forsake the Object of your dearest Affection.

If I find these Hardships unsupportable, replied the *Lover*, believe me I will return in a little time. If I do not, be assured that I am happy, and let the Consciousness of that make you so also. After they had thus reasoned the Case together, they went to their Rest, and meeting the next Morning, the *Lover* being immoveable in his Resolution, took their Leaves of each other, and so parted.

The *Lover* left his Hole, like a Bird that had made his Escape out of a Cage; and as he went on his Journey was ravished with Delight at the Prospect of the Mountains, Rivers and Gardens, which he flew over; and arriving towards Evening at the Foot of a little Hill, where several Rivulets shaded with lovely Trees water'd the enamelled Meadows, he resolved to spend the Night in a Place that so effectually resembled a terrestrial Paradise. But, alas! how soon began he to feel the Vicissitudes of Fortune! Hardly had he betaken himself to his Repose upon a Tree, when the Air grew gloomy, and blazing Gleams of Lightning began to flash against his Eyes, while the Thunder rattled along the Plains, and became doubly terrible by its Echoes from the neighbouring Mountains. The Rain also and the Hail came down together in whole Torrents, and made the poor Pidgeon hop from Bow to Bow, beaten, wetted to the Skin, and in continual Terror of being consumed in a Flash of Lightning. In short, he spent the Night so ill, that he already heartily repented his having left his Comrade.

The next Morning, the Sun having dispersed the Clouds, the *Lover* was prudent enough to take his Leave of the Tree, with a full Resolution to make the best of his Way home again; he had not however flown fifty Yards, when a Sparrow-Hawk, with a keen Appetite, perceiving our Traveller, pursued him upon the Wing. The Pidgeon seeing him at a Distance, began to tremble; and as he approached nearer, utterly despairing ever to see his Friend again, and no less sorry that he had not followed her Advice, protested, that, if ever he escaped that Danger, he would never more think of travelling. In this time the Sparrow-Hawk had overtaken, and was just ready to seize him, and tear him in Pieces, when a hungry Eagle lancing down with a full Stoop upon the Sparrow-Hawk, cried out, Hold, let me devour that Pidgeon to stay my Stomach, till I find something else more solid. The Sparrow-Hawk however no less courageous than hungry, would not, tho' unequal in Strength, give way to the Eagle: so that the two Birds of Prey fell to fighting one with another, and in the mean time the poor Pidgeon escaped, and perceiving a Hole so small that it would hardly give Entrance to a Titmouse, yet made shift to squeeze himself into it, and so spent the Night in a World of Fear and Trouble. By break of Day he got out again, but he was now become so weak for want of Food, that he could hardly fly: add to this, he had not yet half recovered himself from the Fear he was in the Day before: As he was however full of Terror, looking round about him to see whether the Sparrow-Hawk or the Eagle appeared, he spied a Pidgeon in a Field, at a small Distance, with a great deal of Corn scattered in the Place where he was feeding. The *Lover*, rejoiced at the Sight, drew near this happy Pidgeon, as he thought him, and without Compliments fell to: But he had hardy pecked three Grains before he found himself caught by the Legs. *The Pleasures of this World indeed are generally but Snares which the Devil lays for us.*

Brother, said the *Lover* to the other Pidgeon, we are both of one and the same Species; wherefore then did you not inform me of this Piece of Treachery, that I might not have fallen into these Springes they have laid for us. To which the other answered, Forbear Complaints, no body can prevent his Destiny; nor can all the Prudence of Man preserve him from inevitable Accidents. The *Lover* on this next besought him to teach him some Expedient to free himself from the Danger that threatened him. Poor innocent Creature, answered the other, if I knew any means to do this, dost thou not think I would make use of it to deliver myself, that so I might not be the Occasion of surprising others of my Fellow-creatures? Alas! unfortunate Friend, thou art but like the young Camel, who, weary with travelling, cried to his Mother with Tears in his Eyes, O Mother without Affection! stop a little, that I may take Breath and rest myself. To whom the Mother replied, O Son without Consideration! seest thou not that my Bridle is in the Hand of another? Were I at Liberty, I would gladly both throw down by Burden, and give thee my Assistance: But alas! we must both submit to what we cannot avoid or prevent. Our Traveller perceiving, by this Discourse, that all Hopes of Relief from others were vain, resolved to rely only on himself, and strengthened by his own Despair, with much striving and long fluttering at length broke the Snare, and taking the Benefit of his unexpected good Fortune, bent his Flight toward his own Country; and such was his Joy for having escaped so great a Danger, that he even forgot his Hunger. However at length passing through a Village, and lighting, meerly for a little Rest, upon a Wall that was over-against a Field newly sown, a Countryman that was keeping the Birds from his Corn, perceiving the Pidgeon, flung a Stone at him, and while the poor *Lover* was dreaming of nothing less than of the Harm that was so near him, hit him so terrible a Blow that he fell quite stunn'd into a deep and dry Well that was at the Foot of the Wall. By this however he escaped being made the Countryman's Supper, who not being able to come at his

Prey, left it in the Well, and never thought more of it. There the Pidgeon remained all the Night long in the Well with a sad Heart, and a Wing half broken. During the Night his Misfortunes would not permit him to sleep, and a thousand and a thousand times he wished himself at home with his Friend: the next Day, however, he so bestir'd himself, that he got out of the Well, and towards Evening arrived at his old Habitation.

The *Beloved* hearing the fluttering of her Companion's Wings, flew forth with a more than ordinary Joy to meet him; but seeing him so weak and in so bad a Condition, asked him tenderly the reason of it: Upon which the *Lover* told her all his Adventures, protesting heartily to take her Advice for the future, and never to travel more.

I have recited, concluded the Vizir, this Example to your Majesty, to dissuade you from preferring the Inconveniences of travelling to the Repose that you enjoy at home, among the Praises and Adorations of a loyal and happy People. Wise Vizir, said the King, I acknowledge it a painful thing to travel; but it is no less true, that there is great and useful Knowledge to be gained by it. Should a Man be always tied to his own House or his own Country, he would be deprived the Sight and Enjoyment of an infinite Number of noble Things. And to continue your allegoric History of Birds, the Falcon is happy in seeing the Beauties of the World, while Princes frequently carry them upon their Hands, and for that Honour and Pleasure he quits the inglorious Life of the Nest. On the other hand, the Owl is contemned, because he always hides himself in ruinous Buildings and dark Holes, and delights in nothing but Retirement. The Mind of Man ought to fly abroad and soar like the Falcon, not hide itself like the Owl. He that travels renders himself acceptable to all the World, and Men of Wisdom and Learning are pleased with his Conversation. Nothing is more clear and limpid than running Water, while stagnating Puddles grow thick and muddy. Had the famous Falcon, that was bred in the Raven's Nest, never flown abroad, he would never have been so highly advanced. *The Vizir on this humbly besought the King to recite that Fable, which he did in the following Manner.*

FABLE II.

The FALCON and the RAVEN.

THERE were once two Falcons which had built their Nests near one another in a very high Mountain, from whence they flew every way round them to seek Food for their young Ones. One Day as they were flown abroad upon the fame Design, they staid from their Nests a little too long; for, in the mean time, one of the young ones, very hungry, put his Head so far out of the Nest to look for them, that he tumbled over, and fell from the Top to the Foot of the Mountain; at this Instant a Raven that happened to be in that part met with the fallen Youngling, and at first took it for a Rat which some other Raven had accidentally let fall; but, on more Examination, finding by his Beak and his Talons that he was a Bird of Prey, he began to have kindness for him; and looking upon himself as a Instrument ordained by Heaven to save the helpless Creature, carried it to his own Nest, and bred it up with his own young ones, where the Falcon grew every Day bigger and bigger, and, coming at length to be of Age to make Reflections, nobly began to say to himself, If I am Brother to these Ravens, why am I not made as they are? And if I am not of their Race and Progeny, why to I tarry here? One Day as he was taken up with these Meditations, "Son, said the Raven to him, I have observed thee for some time to be very sad and pensive; I conjure thee, let me know the Cause of it: If any thing grieve thee, conceal it not from me, for I will endeavour thy Relief and Consolation." "I know not myself, replied the Falcon, the Reason of my Desires, but I have long resolved to beg your Permission to travel." "Oh Son, cried the Raven, thou art forming a Design in thy young Imagination, which my riper Years can inform thee, will create in thee an infinite deal of Pains and Danger. *Travelling is a Sea that swallows up all the World.* Wise People, however, never travel, unless it be either to get great Estates, or because they cannot live contented and easy at home: Neither of these two Reasons, Thanks to Heaven, can, I think, have infused this Design into the Brain, because thou wantest for nothing, and why therefore wouldst thou leave us ? Thou hast the absolute Power over thy Brothers and Sisters, and all that I can do for thee thou need'st but command. It is a great Folly, therefore, in thee to quit an assured Repose at home, to ramble in search of Trouble and Disquiet in foreign Countries." To this the Falcon replied, "Sir, what you tell me is most true, and I take it as a Demonstration of your paternal Kindness for me; but I feel something within me, which persuades me that I lead a life here in this Place, not worthy of myself." The Raven on this could not but observe, that in despite of a bad Eductation, Persons nobly descended are still the Masters of Sentiments becoming their Birth. He would fain, however, have put him upon farther Discourse, in hopes to wean him from this strong Inclination to travel; and to that Purpose, "Son, said he, my Exhortations are Persuasions to Sobriety and Contentedness; but those high soaring Thoughts of thine, are only the Effects of Avarice. And let me assure thee of this, *that whoever is not contented with what be has, can never be at quiet in his Mind;* and I am in the highest Degree concerned to find thou art not satisfied with thy Condition; but take with thee this my friendly Admonition: Beware lest what once befel the greedy and ambitious Cat should happen to thee also." *The Story is this.*

F A B L E III.

The greedy and ambitious CAT.

THERE was formerly an old Woman in a Village, extremely thin, half-starved, and meagre. She lived in a little Cottage as dark and gloomy as a Fool's Heart, and withal as close shut up as a Miser's Hand. This miserable Creature had for the Companion of her wretched Retirements a Cat meagre and lean as herself; the poor Creature never saw Bread, nor beheld the Face of a Stranger, and was forced to be contented with only smelling the Mice in their Holes, or seeing the Prints of their Feet in the Dust. If by some extraordinary lucky Chance this miserable Animal happened to catch a Mouse, she was like a Beggar that discovers a Treasure; her Visage and her Eyes were enflamed with Joy, and that Booty served her for a whole Week; and out of the Excess of her Admiration, and Distrust of her own Happiness, she would cry out to herself, Heavens! Is this a Dream, or is it real? One Day, however, ready to die for Hunger, she got upon the Ridge of her enchanted Castle, which had long been the Mansion of Famine for Cats, and spied from thence another Cat, that was stalking upon a Neighbour's Wall like a Lion, walking along as if she had been counting her Steps, and so fat that she could hardly go. The old Woman's Cat, astonished to see a Creature of her own Species, so plump and so large, with a loud Voice cries out to her pursy Neighbour, In the Name of Pity, *Speak to me, thou happiest of the Cat-kind!* Why, you look as if you came from one of the Khan* of *Kathai's* Feasts; I conjure you, to tell me how, or in what Region it is that you get your Skin so well stuffed? Where! replied the fat One. Why, where should one feed well but at a King's Table? I go to the House, continued she, every Day about Dinner-time, and there I lay my Paws upon some delicious Morsel or other, which serves me till the next, and then leave enough for an Army of Mice, which under me live in Peace and Tranquility; for why should I commit Murder for a Piece of tough and skinny Mouse-flesh, when I can live on Venison at a much easier Rate. The lean Cat on this eagerly enquired the way to this House of Plenty, and entreated her plump Neighbour to carry her one Day along with her. Most willingly, said the fat Puss, for thou feest I am naturally charitable, and thou art so lean that I heartily pity thy Condition. On this Promise they parted; and the lean Cat returned to the old Woman's Chamber, where she told her Dame the Story of what had befallen her. The old Woman prudently endeavoured to dissuade her Cat from prosecuting her Design, admonishing her withal to have a Care of being deceived; for, believe me, said she, *the Desires of the Ambitious are never to be satiated, but when their Mouths are stuffed with the Dirt of their Graves.* Sobriety and Temperance are the only Things that truly enrich People. I must tell thee, poor silly Cat, that they who travel to satisfy their Ambition, have no Knowledge of the good Things they possess, *nor are they truly thankful to Heaven for what they enjoy, who are not contented with their Fortune.*

The poor starved Cat, however, had conceived so fair an Idea of the King's Table, that the old Woman's good Morals, and judicious Remonstrances, entered in at one Ear and went out at the other: in short, she departed the next Day with the fat Puss to go to the King's House. But alas! before she got thither, her Destiny had laid a Snare for her: For, being a House of good Cheer, it was so haunted with

---

* A Nobleman of the East, famous for his Hospitality.

Cats, that the Servants had, just at this Time, Orders to kill all the Cats that came near it, by reason of a great Robbery committed the Night before in the King's Larder by several Grimalkins. The old Woman's Cat, however, pushed on by Hunger, entered the House, and no sooner saw a Dish of Meat unobserved by the Cooks, but she made a Seizure of it, and was doing what for many Years she had not done before, that is, heartily filling her Belly; but as she was enjoying herself under the Dresser-board, and feeding heartily upon her stolen Morsels, one of the testy Officers of the Kitchen, missing his Breakfast, and seeing where the poor Cat was solacing herself with it, threw his Knife at her with such an unlucky Hand, that he stuck her full in the Breast. However, as it has been the Providence of Nature to give this Creature nine Lives instead of one, poor Puss made a Shift to crawl away, after she had for some time shammed dead: But, in her Flight, observing the Blood come streaming from her Wound; well, said she, let me but escape this Accident, and if ever I quit my old Hold and my own Mice for all the Rarities in the King's Kitchen, may I lose all my nine Lives at once.

I cite you this Example, to shew you, that it is better to be contented with what one has, than to travel in search of what Ambition prompts us to seek for. What you say, said the Falcon, is true, and it is a very wholsome Advice; but it is for mean and low Spirits only to confine themselves always to a little Hole. He that aspires to be a King, must begin with the Conquest of a Kingdom, and he that would meet a Crown, must go in search of it. An effeminate and lazy Life can never agree with a great Soul.

You are very magnanimous, Son, replied the Raven, and I perceive design great Conquests; but let me tell you, your Enterprize cannot so soon be put in Execution: before you can conquer a Kingdom, you must get together Arms and Armies, and make great Preparations. My Talons, replied the Falcon, are Instruments sufficient to bring about my Design, and myself am equal to the Undertaking. Sure you never heard the Story of the Warrior, who by his single Valour became a King. No, replied the Raven, therefore let me hear it from you: On which the Falcon related it in this Manner.

FABLE IV.

The Poor Man *who became a* Great King.

It being the Pleasure of Heaven to rescue from Misery a Man who lived in extreme Poverty, Providence gave him a Son, who from his Infancy shewed evident Signs, that he would one Day come to be a great Man. This Infant became an immediate Blessing to the old Man's House, for his Wealth increased from Day to Day, from the Time that the Child was born. So soon as this young One could speak, he talked of nothing but Swords, and Bows and Arrows. The Father sent him to School, and did all he could to infuse into him a good Relish for Learning; but he neglected his Book, and devoted his Thoughts to nothing but running at the Ring, and other warlike Exercises, with the other Children.

When he came to Years of Discretion, "Son, said his Father to him, thou art now past the Age of Childhood, and art in the greatest Danger to fall into Disorder and Irregularity, if thou givest thyself over to thy Passions. I therefore intend to prevent that Accident by marrying thee betimes." "Dear Father, replied the Stripling, for Heaven's Sake refuse me not the Mistress which my youthful Years have already made choice of." "Who is that Mistress?"

presently replied the old Man, with great Earnestness and Uneasiness (for he had already looked out for him the Daughter of a neighbouring Hind, and agreed the Matter with her Father) "and what is her Condition?" "This is she, the Lad made Answer, shewing his Father a very noble Sword; and by Virtue of this I expect to become Master of a Throne." The Father gave him many Reasons to imagine he disapproved his Intentions, and looked on them as little better than Madness: Many a good Lecture followed during the Remainder of the Day; to avoid which for the future, the young Hero the next Morning quitted his Father's House, and travelled in search of Opportunities to signalize his Courage. Many Years he warred under the Command of different Monarchs: At length, after he had every-where signalized himself, not only by his Conduct, but by his personal Courage, a neighbouring Monarch, who, with his whole Family, lay besieged in a small Fortress, sent to him to intreat him to accept of the Command of all his Forces, to get them together, and endeavour to raise the Siege, and relieve them; in which, if he succeeded, he would make him his adopted Son, and the Heir of his vast Empire. Our Young Warrior engaged in this, raised a vast Army, fought the Besiegers in their Trenches, entirely conquered them, and was the Gainer of a glorious Victory: But, alas! the Heat of the Action made him not perceive that the Fortress in which the King was, was in Flames; some treacherous Person had fired it, at the Instigation of the General of the Besieger's Army, and the King and his whole Family perished in the Flames: the old Monarch just lived, however, to see his Deliverer, and to settle on him the Inheritance of his Crown. The Royal Family being all extinct by this fatal Calamity, the Nobles ratified the Grant, and our illustrious Hero lived many Years a great and glorious Monarch.

I have recited this Example, said the Falcon to the Raven, that you may understand that I also find myself born to undertake great Enterprizes: I have a strange forboding within me, that I shall prove no less fortunate than this famous Warrior; and for this Reason can never quit my Design. When the Raven perceived him so fixed in his Resolution, he consented to his putting it in Execution; persuaded that so noble a Courage would never be guilty of idle or unworthy Actions.

The Falcon having taken his Leave of the Raven, and bid Farewel to all his pretended Brethren, left the Nest and flew away. Long he continued flying, and in Love with Liberty, and at length stopt upon a Mountain: here, looking round about him, he spied a Partridge in the fallow Grounds, that made all the neighbouring Hills resound with her Note. Presently the Falcon lanced himself upon her, and having got her in his Pounce, began to tear and eat her. This is no bad Beginning, said he to himself; though it were for nothing but to taste such delicate Food, 'tis better travelling than to lie sleeping in a nasty Nest, and feed upon Carrion, as my Brothers do. Thus he spent three Days in feasting himself with delicate Morsels; but on the fourth, being on the Top of another Mountain, he saw a Company of Men that were hawking: these happened to be the King of the Country with all his Court; and while he was gazing upon them, he saw their Falcon in pursuit of a Heron. Upon that, pricked forward by a noble Emulation, he flies with all his Force, gets before the King's Falcon, and overtakes the Heron. The King admiring this Agility, commands his Falconers to make use of all their Cunning to catch this noble Bird, which by good Luck they did. And in a little Time he so entirely won the Affection of the King, that he did him the Honour to carry him usually upon his own Hand.

Had he always staid in his Nest, concluded the Monarch, this good Fortune had never befallen him. And you see, by this Fable, that it is no unprofitable Thing to travel. It rouses the Genius of People, and renders them capable of noble Atchievements. *Dabschelim* having ended his Discourse, the Vizir, after he had made his Submissions, and paid his Duty according to Custom, came forward, and addressing himself to the King, said, "Sir, what your Majesty has said is most true; but I cannot but think yet that it is not adviseable that a great, a glorious, and happy King, should quit his Repose for the Hardship and Danger of travelling." "Men of Courage, answered the King, delight in Labour, Fatigue, and Danger. If Kings, who have Power, strip not the Thorns from the Rose-bushes, the Poor can never gather the Roses; and till Princes have endured the Inconveniencies of Campaigns, the People can never sleep in Peace. No body can be safe in these Dominions, while thou seekest nothing but my Ease. He that travels meets with Rest, and every thing else that he desires, like the Leopard, who by his Pains and Diligence, and despising the Fatigues of travelling, acquired what he wished for. Upon this, the Vizir humbly besought the King to relate that Fable to his Slave: which he did in these Words.

FABLE V.

The LEOPARD and the LION.

IN the Neighbourhood of *Bassora*, there was a very lovely Island, in which grew a most delightful Wood, where pleasing Breezes whispered their Love Stories to the rustling Leaves. This enchanting Forest was watered with several Fountains, whence a Number of recreating Streams ran gently winding to every Part of it. In this lovely Place there lodged a Leopard, so furious, that even the most daring Lions durst not approach within a League of his Habitation. For several Years his renowned and unequalled Courage kept him in Peace within this Island, with a little Leopard that was his favourite and Heir: To whom, said he, one Day, "Son, so soon as thou shalt be strong enough to oppose my Enemies, I will resign to thee the Care of governing this Island, and retire into one Corner of it, where I will spend the Remainder of my Days, without Trouble or Molestation." But Death crossed the old Leopard's Design: He died when he least dreamt of it; and the young One, before he expected it, succeeded him. The ancient Enemies of the old Leopard had no sooner heard of his Death, and the Weakness of his Successor, but they entered into a League, and together invaded the Island; and the young Leopard, finding himself unable to withstand such a Number of Enemies, made his escape into the Desarts, and there secured himself. In the mean time his Enemies, having together made themselves Masters of the Island, every one claimed an equal Right to the Sovereignty, and each would command in Chief. Thus they fell out, and the Business came to the Decision of a bloody Battle, wherein the Lion being Victor, drove all the rest of his Competitors out of his Territories, and he became the sole and peaceable Master of the Island.

Some Years after, the Leopard having devoted his Life to Travel, in one of his Journies meeting an assembled Body of Lions in a remote Part of the Forest, recounted to them his Misfortunes, and besought them to assist him in the Recovery of his just Inheritance. But the Lions, who knew full well the Strength of the Usurper, refused their Assistance to the Leopard, and replied, "Poor silly Creature! dost thou not understand that thy Island is now under the Power of a Lion so redoubted, that the very Birds are afraid to fly over his Head? We advise thee rather, added they, to go and wait upon him; submissively offer thy Services to him, and take some lucky Opportunity privately to revenge the Injuries he has done thee." The Leopard followed this Counsel, went to the Lion's Court, and there intruding himself into the Acquaintance of one of the most favourite Domestics, by a thousand Caresses engaged him to give him an Opportunity to discourse with his Master. When he had obtained Permission, he played his Part so well that the Lion judged him to be a Creature of much Merit, and conferred a very noble Employment upon him in his Court. In a very litte Time, the Leopard so infinuated himself into the Lion's Favour, that the first Grandees of the Court began to grow jealous of him. But their Jealousies were all in vain, the Lion found him more valuable than them all, and inspite of all their idle Malice, treated him accordingly. It happened some Time after this, that some extraordinary Exigence of State called away the Lion to a Place far distant from the Island: but the Monarch, being now grown lazy, had no mind to stir out of his delightful Abode at a Time that the Heat was so excessive. This the Leopard perceiving, offered to undertake the Voyage himself; and, after he had obtained Leave, departed; arrived at the Place, dispatched his Business, and returned back to Court with such an unexpected Speed, that the King, admiring his Diligence, said to those about him, "This Leopard is one whom it is impossible for me sufficiently to reward; he contemns Labour, and despises Hardship, so it be to procure the Welfare and Peace of my Dominions". Having said this, he sent for the Leopard, highly applauded his Zeal, and in Reward of his Services gave him the Government of all his Forrests, and made him his Heir. Now, Vizir, had not the Leopard undertaken his Journey, he had never regained his Island.

The Minister now finding that it would be impossible to dissuade the King from the Resolution he had taken to travel, said no more to hinder him, and he soon prepared for his Journey. During his Absence he intrusted those Vizirs, in whom he had the greatest Confidence, with the Care of his Dominions, and charged them above all Things to be kind and loving to the People. After a thousand Admonitions of this kind, and a strict Care that none but People worthy their Office were left in Trust till his Return, the gorious *Dabschelim*, being at Ease with himself, and in full Peace of Mind, set forward with some of his Courtiers for *Serandib*; where he at length safely arrived, after a long and painful Journey. When he had given himself the Refreshment of a short Repose, he began to think of the Business of his Journey. He spent first however three Days in walking about and taking a full View of the City; then leaving his most cumbersome Baggage behind, as also some Part of his Train, he crossed the Mountain, which he found wonderfully high and steep, but environed with a great Number of pleasant Gardens and lovely Meadows. When he had now crossed the Mountain and was descending on the other Side, he perceived a very obscure Den or Cavern, which, on his Enquiry, the Inhabitants of the Mountain, told him was the Retirement of a certain Hermit, called *Bidpay*, that is to say, the *friendly Physician*; and that some of the *Indian* Grandees called him *Pilpay*: that he was a Person of profound Knowledge, and had retired from the World in Contempt of the Hurry and Vanity of it, and pleased himself in leading a solitary Life. This highly increased *Dabschelim's* Curiosity, who therefore went himself to the Mouth of the Cave; and *Pilpay*, seeing him approach, went

out to meet him, and invited him in. The King being
entered, the old *Bramin* besought him to rest himself, and
begged leave to ask him the Reason of his taking so long and
dangerous a Journey. The King, who had something of a
prophetic Apprehension that he should meet with what he
sought for in his Converse with this old Man, recounted to
him the whole Story of his Travels, his Dream, the
Discovery of the Treasure, and what was contained in the
piece of white Sattin. The *Bramin* then, with a Look of the
highest Pleasure, told the King, he looked upon those to be
a happy People who lived under his Reign, and that he
could not sufficiently applaud his having contemned the
Fatigues of a tedious Journey, to acquire Knowledge for the
Felicity of his Subjects. Then taking Occasion from hence,
he opened his Lips like a Cabinet of precious Knowledge,
and charmed *Dabschelim* with his admirable Discourses.
After several other Things they talked concerning
Houschenk's Letter. *Dabschelim* read the Admonitions which
it contained one after the other: At the End of each *Pilpay*
gave the Fables which served to illustrate them, and the
Monarch heedfully kept them in his Memory.

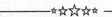

C H A P. II.

That we ought to avoid the Insinuations of FLATTERS *and* BACKBITERS.

THE first Admonition, said the Monarch to the *Bramin*, contained in this most inestimable Legacy of moral Precepts, is, *That Kings ought never to listen to false Reports, or the insinuating Malice of Flatters, which never produce any Thing but Misfortunes, and always bring an ill End to such as hearken to them.* Whoever, cried the *Bramin*, observes not this Command, must needs be ignorant of the Fable of the *Lion and the Ox*. Upon which the King being desirous to hear it, *Pilpay* in the following Manner began the Fable.

F A B L E I.

The MERCHANT *and his* LEWD CHILDREN; *being the Introduction to the Fable of the* LION *and the* OX.

A CERTAIN Merchant, a Man well skilled in the Affairs of the world, falling sick, and perceiving that his Age and his Distemper would not long permit him to live, called his three Sons together, who were very debauched, and wasted his Estate in Riot and Disorder. "Sons, said he, I know you may be in some measure excused for thus consuming my Estate, inasmuch as that you know not what it cost to get it: But it becomes you to learn, at least, that Riches should be only properly made instrumental to acquire the Blessings of Heaven and Earth. There are three Things that Men of different Tempers and Dispositions labour for in this World with more than ordinary Vehemence. The first is, to enjoy all the Pleasures of Life; and the Seekers-after these are the People who are addicted to Intemperance, and abandon themselves to sensual Delights. The second is, to obtain high Dignities and Preserments: Those who endeavour after these are the Ambitious, who only love to command and be admired. The third is, to acquire more valuable and more lasting Joys, the Joys of Heaven; and to take Delight in doing Good to others. Those who place their Happiness in these noble Enjoyments, deserve the highest Admiration and Applauses. But, my Sons, there is no way to attain this last great End, but by the Means of Wealth well got. Now seeing that what we seek for in this World is not to be had without Money; *That*, as it can procure us whatever we search for, must be first of all acquired, and most carefully preserved: But they who meet an Estate already got to their Hands, know not the Trouble of getting it, and that's the Reason they consume it so prodigally. Therefore, dear Children, give over this irregular Life, take care of yourselves, and rather endeavour to increase your Estates, than to waste them in there idle Extravagancies." "Father, replied the eldest Son, you command us to acquire; but you should consider that Acquisition depends only upon Fortune. This also I am perfectly convinced of, that we shall never want what is destined us, tho' we should never stir a Foot to obtain it: On the other Side, we shall never be Masters of what is not ordained for us, though we should torment ourselves to Death in the endeavouring after it. I remember an old Proverb: *Whenever I fled what Destiny had allotted, I always met with it; but whenever I sought for that which never was appointed me, I never could find it.* This is clearly to be seen by the Fable of the old King's two Sons; of which, one discovered his Father's Treasures, and gained the Kingdom with little Trouble, while the other lost it, though he did all he could to preserve it. The Father on this desired that he might hear this Story: which his Son rehearsed as follows.

F A B L E II.

The KING *and his* TWO SONS.

IN The Country of *Ardos,** there lived an ancient King who
had two Sons, both covetous, yet given to Debauchery. This
Monarch finding the Infirmities of Age increase upon him,
and that he was hasting to the other World, and considering
the Humour of his two Sons, was much afraid that after his
Death they would dissipate in idle Expences the vast
Treasure which he had heaped together, and therefore
resolved to hide it. With this Design he went to a religious
Hermit who had retired from the World, and in whom he
had a very great Confidence. By the Counsel of this Hermit,
the Treasure was buried in the Earth near where the
Hermit dwelt, so privately that no body knew any thing of it.
This done, the King made his Will, which he put into the
Hermit's Hands, with these farther Orders: "I charge you,
said he, to reveal this Treasure to my Children, when, after
my Death you see them in the Distresses of Poverty. It may
be, added the King, that when they have suffered a little

---

* *Ardos* is a Province to the North-East of the River *Indus.*

Hardship, they will become more prudent in their Conduct."

The Hermit having promised all Fidelity in the Observance of the King's Commands, the Monarch returned to his Palace, and in a short Time after died; nor did the Hermit long survive him: The Treasure therefore lay concealed, probably for ever to continue so, in the Hermitage. The King being now dead, the Sons could not agree about the Succession. This occasioned a bloody War between them; and the eldest, who was the more powerful, utterly despoiled his younger Brother of all that he had. This young Prince, thus deprived of his Inheritance, fell into a deep Melancholy, and resolved to quit the World. To that Purpose he left the City, and calling to mind the Kindness between his Father and the Hermit, "There is no other Way for me, said he to himself, but to find out this honest Man, that I may learn of him to live as he does, and end my Life in Peace and Contentedness in his Company." With this Resolution he left the City, but coming to the Hermitage, found that the Hermit was dead. He was greatly afflicted and disappointed at this unexpected Chance; but at length came to a Resolution to live as he had done; and accordingly made choice of his Retirement for his Habitation.

Now there was in this Hermitage a Well, which had been used to supply the Place with Water, but it was now dry: to enquire into the Cause of this, the unhappy Prince ventured to let himself down to the Bottom of the Well. But how great was his Astonishment, when he saw the lower Part of it for a great Depth filled with his Father's Treasures! On finding this he was thankful to Heaven, and wisely took up a Resolution to lay out his Money with more Moderation than he had done before.

On the other hand, his Brother, who sat securely revelling upon his Throne without any Care of his People or his Army, imagining with himself that his Father's Treasure was hid in the Palace, as he had told him upon his Death-bed; one Day, being at War with a neighbouring Prince, was obliged to have recourse to his expected Treasure. But how was he amazed, after he had sought a long time and found nothing! This quite disabled him from raising a powerful Army, and threw him into a very great Fit of Melancholy. However, making a Virtue of Necessity, he raised what Force he could, and marched out of the City to meet and encounter his Enemy. The Battle was obstinate, and this King and his Enemy were both slain: so that the two Armies, enraged at the Loss of their Leaders, fell to butcher each other with equal Fury; till at length the Generals having agreed together, that it would be their better Way to chuse a mild and gentle King for the Government of the State, went and found out the young Prince, who was retired to the Hermitage, conducted him in great Pomp to the Royal Palace, and set him upon the Throne.

This Fable shews, that it is better for Men to rely upon Providence, than to torment themselves about the Acquisition of a Thing that was never ordained them. When the young Man had ended his Fable, All this, said the Father, may be true; but all Effects have their Causes, and he who relies upon Providence without considering these, had need to be instructed by the ensuing Fable.

F A B L E III.

The DERVISE, the FALCON, and the RAVEN.

A CERTAIN Dervise used to relate, that in his Youth once passing through a Wood, and admiring the Works of the great Author of Nature, he spied a Falcon that held a Piece of Flesh in his Beak; and hovering about a Tree, tore the Flesh into Bits, and gave it to a young Raven that lay bald and featherless in its Nest. The Dervise admiring the Bounty of Providence, in a Rapture of Admiration cried out, Behold this poor Bird, that is not able to seek out Sustenance for himself, is not however forsaken of its Creator, who spreads the whole World like a Table, where all Creatures have their Food ready provided for them. He extends his Liberality so far, that the Serpent finds wherewith to live upon the Mountain of *Gahen.** Why then am I so greedy, and wherefore do I run to the Ends of the Earth, and plow up the Ocean for Bread? Is it not better than I should henceforward confine myself in Repose to some little Corner, and abandon myself to Fortune. Upon this he retired to his Cell; where, without putting himself to any farther Trouble for any Thing in the World, he remained three Days and three Nights with Victuals. At last, "Servant of mine, said the Creator to him in a Dream, know thou that all things in this World have their Causes: And though my Providence can never be limited, my Wisdom requires that Men shall make use of the Means that I have ordained them. If thou wouldst imitate any one of the Birds thou hast seen, to my Glory, use the Talents I have given thee, and imitate the Falcon that feeds the Raven, and not the Raven that lies a Sluggard in his Nest, and expects his Food from another.

This Example shews us, that we are not to lead idle and lazy Lives upon the Pretence of depending upon Providence. On this, the elder Son was silenced; but the second Son, taking upon him to speak, said to his Father, "You advise us, Sir, to labour, and get Estates and Riches; but when we have heaped up a great deal of Wealth, it is not also necessary that you inform us what we shall do with it?"

* A Mountain in the East, famous for a vast Number of venomous Animals.

"Tiseasy to acquire Wealth, replied the Father, but a difficult Thing to expend it well. Riches many Times prove very fatal; an Instance of which you may see in the following Fable."

F A B L E IV.

The COUNTRYMAN *and several* RATS.

THERE was once a certain Husbandman who had a Barn full
of Corn, which he carefully kept close locked up. Not far
from this lived a Rat, who long laboured on every Side of it,
endeavouring to make a Hole somewhere to creep in at.
After great Troubie, he at length found his Way into the
Barn; where when he had thoroughly filled his Belly,
amazed at the vast Treasures which he saw himself Master
of, away he ran, full of Joy, and gave Notice of it to a
Multitude of other Rats, his Neighbours; telling them of his
immense Riches, but carefully concealing the Place where
they lay. On the News of his good Fortune, all the Rats of
the neighbouring Villages presently flocked about him, and
made him a thousand Offers of their Service, scraping and
cringing to him, and soothing him in all the Excursions of
his fantastic Humour. The Fool, taking all this for Reality,
grew very proud and stately, as believing himself to be some
extraordinary Person; and, never considering that this
Magazine was not to last always, began most extravagantly
to play the Prodigal at the poor Husbandman's Cost,

treating his Companions and Flatterers every Day with as much as they could cram down. At this Juncture of Time there happened in the same Country so terrible a Famine, that the Poor cried out for Bread while the Rat lay wallowing in Plenty. The Husbandman now believing it his time to make the best of his Corn, opened his Barn Door; but finding a most unexpected Consumption of his Store, he fell into a Passion, and presently removed what he had to another Place. The Rat, who looked upon himself to be sole Master of Mis-rule in the Barn, was then asleep, but his Parasites were awake, and seeing the Husbandman go and come, soon began to fear there was something the Matter, and that they should by and by be murdered for their monstrous Robberies. Upon this they betook themselves every one to Flight, leaving the poor cullied Rat fast asleep, not one of them having Gratitude enough to give him the least Hint of the Danger that threatened him. This is the Practice of your smell-feast Friends: While you keep a plentiful Table they are your most humble and obedient Servants, but when the Accommodation fails, like Tartars they seek for other Pastures, and leave you to Destruction.

The Rat, however, soon after waking, was amazed to find none of his Pick-thanks at his Elbow. He left his Hole in great Haste, to know the Cause; which he too soon found out; for going to the Barn, and finding all was gone, not so much being left as would suffice him for that Day, he fell into such a deep Despair, that in Anger and Distraction, he beat out his Brains against the next Wall, and so ended his Days. This Example, Son, shews that we ought to live according to our Income.

The second Brother being silenced also by this Story, the youngest, taking his Turn, said, "Father, you have well instructed us how to gain Money, and to guard against the foolish wasting it; but now pray inform us, when we have acquired this Wealth you speak of, what is to be done with it." "It is to be made use of, replied the Father, upon all just Occasions; but more especially for the Conveniencies of Life, according to the Rules of Temperance and Justice. In the first Place, your Expences ought not to be such, as afterwards to be repented of by yourselves, or condemned by others, as the Waste of Prodigality: And in the second, it is a good general Rule against the other Extreme, that no

Man ought by his Avarice to render himself hateful to the World."

The Father having thus exhorted his Children to follow his Counsel, they betook themselves all three to particular Callings. The eldest of them turned Merchant, and travelled into foreign Countries. Among other Goods which he purchased for the Sake of Trade, he had two Oxen; both the Calves of the same Cow, and both very fair and beautiful: the one was called *Cohotorbe*, and the other *Mandebe*. Our Merchant took great Care to feed up these Oxen; but because his Journey was long, they, in spite of their good Feeding, before they arrived at the End of it, grew to be weak and lean. While they were in this poor condition they met with a Quagmire in the Road, into which *Cohotorbe* fell, and stuck so fast, that the Merchant had much ado to get him out again; and even when he had got him out, he found the poor Beast was so weak, that, being hardly able to stand, he was forced to leave him behind with another Man, till he could recover Strength to continue his Journey: This Man, after he had kept him three Days in the Desart, grew weary of his Charge, left *Cohotorbe* to feed by himself, and sent the Merchant Word that his Ox was dead. In a little Time after, *Mandebe* died of Overfatigue; and *Cohotorbe* having now a little recovered his Flesh, began to enjoy his Liberty, and ramble from one Place to another; and coming at length into a Meadow that pleased him very well, stayed there for some Time, living in Ease and Plenty; so that he became, in a little more Time, as fair and plump as ever he was before.

Not far from this Meadow there dwelt, unknown to *Cohotorbe*, a Lion, who made all the Inhabitants of the Woods round about him tremble, and commanded over several other Lions, who believed him to be the most potent Sovereign in the World. This powerful Monarch of the Beasts, near whom nothing of the Beef-kind had ever ventured to approach, when he heard the bellowing of our Ox, which was a Noise he had never heard before, a most dreadful Terror seized him, and no Motive could fetch him from his Den to face this unknown Enemy. Ashamed, however to discover his Fears to his Courtiers, he pretended an Illness that made him unable to stir out of his Palace. This King of the Woods, among the rest of his domestic

Servants, had two Foxes that were as cunning as two Crocodiles, one of which was called *Kalila*, and the other *Damna:* these were both Beast of great Intrigue; but the latter, which was the Male, was more proud and more ambitious than the former. One Day, says this inquisitive Fox to his Wife, "Pry'thee, Deary, what is it thinkest thou ails the King, that he dares not walk abroad as he used to do?" To whom *Kalila* answered, "Prythe, Dear, let us never trouble ourselves about these Matters; 'tis sufficient for you and I to live peaceably under his Protection, without examining what he does. 'Tis not for us to prate about State Affairs; and, let me tell you, Spouse, they that meddle with things that no way concern them, are in danger of the same Misfortune that befel the Ape." "And pray, replied the Husband, what was that?" To whom the female Fox made this Reply.

F A B L E V.

The CARPENTER and the APE.

AN Ape, one Day, sat staring upon a Carpenter who was cleaving a Piece of Wood with two Wedges, which he put into the Cleft one after another, as the Split opened. The Carpenter soon after getting away to his dinner, and leaving his work half done, the ape would needs turn Log-cleaver, and coming to the Piece of Wood, pulled out one Wedge, without putting in the other; so that the wood having nothing to keep it asunder, closed immediately again, and catching the meddling fool fast by the two forefeet, there held him till the surly Carpenter returned, who, without Ceremony, knocked him on the Head for meddling with his Work.

"This Fable, Spouse, instructs us, that we ought not to meddle with other People's Business." "Ah, replied *Damna*, but these are but foolish Stories; and let me tell you, 'tis not for those that serve Kings, to be idle: They must be always endeavouring to advance themselves. Know you not the fable of the two companions, one of which, by his Industry, obtained a Crown; while the other, being slothful and faint-hearted, fell into extreme Misery.

F A B L E VI.

The two TRAVELLERS.

THERE were once two Friends, who made a Resolution never to leave each other. In pursuance of this, for a long Time, they always travelled together. But one Day as they were journeying in search of their common Advantages, they came to a deep River at the foot of a Hill; and the Place was so delightful, that they resolved to rest themselves by the Stream. After they were well refreshed, they began to look about them, and please their eyes with what they could discover most curious in so pleasant a Place; and at length cast their eyes upon a white Stone, that contained the following words written in blue Letters.

"Travellers, we have prepared an excellent Banquet for your Welcome; but you must be bold and deserve it before you can obtain it: What you are to do is this: Throw yourselves boldly into this fountain, and swim to the other Side; you shall there meet with a Lion carved in white Stone; this you must take upon your shoulders, and without stopping run with it to the Top of yonder Mountain, never fearing the wild Beast that surround you, nor the Thorns that prick your Feet; for be assured nothing will hurt you:

And as soon as you are got to the top of the Hill, you will immediately find yourselves in Possession of great Felicity: But if you cease going forward, you shall never come to the Happiness; nor shall the slothful ever attain to what is here prepared for the Industrious."

The *Ganem*, for that was the Name of one of the two companions, says to *Salem*, for so was the other called, Brother, here is a Means prescribed us that will put an end to all our Pains and Travel; let us take Courage, and try whether what this Stone contains be true or false. Dear Brother, replied *Salem*, 'tis not for a Man of Sense to give Credit to such an idle Writing as this appears to me to be; and in a vain Expectation of I know not what uncertain Gain, to throw himself into evident Danger. Friend, replied *Ganem*, They who have Courage contemn Danger, to make themselves happy; there is no gathering the Rose, without being pricked by the Thorns. Be that as it will, answered *Salem*, it is but a romantic Valour that prompts us to attempt Enterprizes, the End of which we know not, even though we should succeed: And if we are in our Senses, we must see that it is not our Business, for the Sake of a dark Promise, to throw ourselves into this Water, that seems to be a kind of an Abyss, from whence it may not be so easy to get out again. A rational Man, Brother, never moves one of his Feet till the other be fixed. Perhaps this Writing may be a meer Whimsy, the idle Diversion of some wandering Beggar; or even if it should be real, perhaps when you have crossed this River, this Lion of Stone may prove so heavy, that you may not be able to do as you are ordered, and run with it, without slopping, to the Top of the Mountain. But supposing even that all this were easy for you to perform, yet trust me, 'tis not worth while to attempt it; for when you have done whatever is by you to be done, you know not what will be the issue of your Trouble. For my part, I will be no sharer with you in Dangers of this kind, but shall use all my Rhetorick to endeavour to dissuade you from such idle and chimerical Undertakings. No Persuasions, replied *Ganem*, shall make me alter my resolution: And therefore if you will not follow me, dear Friend, at least be pleased to see me venture. *Salem*, seeing him so resolute, cried out, Dearest Brother, if you are weak enough, in your Reason, to determine on this rash, and to me distracted, Undertaking, give me a last Embrace, and farewel for ever: you have refused my Admonitions, and I have not the power to stay and be a witness of your Ruin. On this they took a parting Embrace, and *Salem*, taking his Leave of his, as he supposed, unhappy Brother, set forward upon his Journey.

On the other hand, *Ganem* went to the Brink of the River, resolving to perish, or to win the Prize. He found it deep, but, strengthened by his courage, he threw himself in, and swam to the other Side. When he had recovered the dry Land, he rested himself a while; and then lifting up the Lion, which he saw before him, with all his Might, ran with it, without stopping, to the Top of the Mountain. When he had reached the Top, he had before him the Prospect of a very fair and glorious City, which, as he was attentively viewing, there issued from the Lion of Stone such a terrible thundering Noise, that the Mountain, and all the Places round about it, trembled. This Noise no sooner reached the Ears of the Inhabitants of the City, but they came running up to *Ganem*, who was not a little astonished to see them: and presently some, that seemed to be superior to the rest in quality and Degree, accosted him with great Respect and Ceremony; and after they had harangued him with many large Encomiums, they set him upon a Horse sumptuously caparisoned, conducted him to the City, where they made him put on the Royal Robes, and proclaimed him King of all their Country. When this Ceremony was over, and the Inhabitants seemed all very well pleased with their King, the new Monarch desired to understand the Reason of his advancement: to which they answered, that the learned Men of the Kingdom had, in regard to the future Happiness of their Country, by Virtue of a Talisman, so charmed the fountain which he had crossed, and the Lion of Stone, which he carried to the Top of the Mountain, that whenever their King died, any one who was so adventurous as to expose himself to the Hazards he had done, and brought the Lion safe to the Top of the Mountain, had this Reward for his courage; that the Lion roared out so prodigiously, that the Inhabitants hearing the Noise went forth in search of the Person who had arrived with it, to make him their King. This custom, pursued they, has been of long continuance, and was meant to ensure us for our King, a Man of Courage and Resolution; and since the Lot has fallen upon your Majesty, your Sovereignty is absolute among us.

I have rehearsed this Fable to you, Spouse, continued the male Fox, to let you understand, that there is no tasting Pleasure without Trouble. But as Courage and Resolution you see are the sure Ways to preferment, I am resolved never to give over till I am one of the greatest Lords in the court. *Kalila* asked her Spouse on this, what Means he intended to make use of to attain his Ends? Why you see, answered *Damna*, that our Sovereign Lord the Lion seems to be seized with Astonishment and great Uneasiness; now I am determined, to attempt at least, to cure him of his Disquiet. How canst thou presume, cried *Kalila*, to give Counsel to a King, that never wert accustomed to the Cabals of Princes? Persons of Wit, replied *Damna*, never want either the Means or Industry to accomplish their Designs. I remember that one Day, a Handicraft Tradesman, who by his Industry and Genious had gained a Kingdom, received a Letter from a neighbouring Prince, wherein he expostulated with the new King after this Manner: *Thou that didst never handle before any other than a Chizzel or a Saw, how dar'st thou presume to govern a Kingdom?* To which the Carpenter returned for Answer, He that gave me Wit enough to guide a Saw, will also give me Judgment to wield a Sword; with which I doubt not but I shall be able to chastise the Insolence of any of my two arrogant Neighbours. I know very well, replied *Kalila*, my Dear, that you have both Genius and Courage; but let me put you in mind, that Kings do not always cherish with their Favours, those who have Wit and Merit to deserve them; but their oldest Servants, and such as have done the State important Service, generally are the People who have the greatest share of their Favours; and as you are but a New-comer, and indeed none of the most eminent of the King's Servants, when you consider this, which, believe me, is the true State of the Case, what can you pretend to? Value me not, replied *Damna*, on the Merit of what I am at Court at present; for let me tell you, I hope, in a short time, to have a much more considerable employment. I well know what are the Methods of ingratiating one's self with great Persons, and let me, for your own Sake, inform you, that they who aspire to be admitted into the Cabinets of Princes, ought to have five particular Qualifications: Which are, *never to be in a Passion; to avoid Pride; not to be covetous; to be sincere; and never too be astonished at the changes of Fortune.* These are very good

Maxims, replied *Kalila*, in all States of Life; but pray tell me, supposing you were advanced to be the King's Favourite, what are the virtues you would practise to keep his Esteem. I would serve him, replied *Damna*, with a perfect Fidelity; I would punctually obey him; and whatever the King does, always believe his Intentions good: I would persuade him to do Good, by laying before him the Benefits he will receive thereby, and dissuade him from doing whatever may be prejudicial to himself or his Kingdom. I find, said *Kalila*, thou art resolved to go on with this Design, and must needs own thou seem'st to have well qualified thyself for it; but yet let me warn thee to have a care what thou do'st, for 'tis a dangerous thing to serve a Prince. Wise Men say, that *there are three Sorts of Persons who are wholly deprived of Judgment: They who are ambitious of Preserments in the courts of Princes: They who make use of Poison, to shew their skill in curing it; and they who enstrust Women with their Secrets.* A King is well compared to a high Mountain upon which there are Mines of precious Stones, and also numerous Herds of wild devouring Beasts: 'Tis a difficult thing to accost these, but more dangerous to inhabit them. Kings are also well compared to a wild Ocean, wherein sea-faring people generally either make their fortunes, or perish. I am not ignorant of all this, replied *Damna* in his turn; but know also, that Kings resemble fire, which will burn those that approach too near it; and let me also tell thee, Wise, that he who is afraid to adventure, will never come to any thing. After this discourse, *Damna* went to wait upon the Lion, and as soon as he approached his Presence, made him a profound Reverence. The Lion took immediate Notice of him, and asked who he was. To which some of his courtiers replied, that he was such a one, and that his Father had a long time served his Majesty. Oh, said the King, I now remember him—then turning to *Damna*, well Friend, said the Monarch very graciously, where do you live?—I supply my Father's Place in your Majesty's Houshold, replied *Damna*, but till now I have never durst presume to appear in your Majesty's Presence with the Offer of my Service. I hope your Majesty will not disdain the Oblation of my faithful. Intentions, though I am the meanest and unworthiest of your Majesty's Servants. Dry Wood is sometimes as much esteemed, as a beautiful Tree. The Lion was much pleased with *Damna's* Eloquence, and looking upon his Courtiers, wit, said he, resembles fire, which will shew itself, though covered with Ashes. *Damna* was so overjoyed that his compliment had pleased the King, that he took his Opportunity to beg a private audience of his Majesty; and when they were together; sir, said *Damna*, first let me implore your Majesty's Pardon, for presuming to speak before your Majesty; and them, if I may presume so far, beseech your Majesty to let me know the Cause of your melancholy Retirement; for within these few Days I have, with great sorrow, observed your Majesty has not been so cheerful as you were wont to be. Fain would the Lion have concealed his Fear, but pleased with *Damna's* winning Behaviour, and wanting some one to unbofom his Grief to, he determined to entrust him with the fatal Secret of his Fears; just as he was about to utter the Cause of his Troubles, behold *Cohotorbe* set up a most terrible bellowing; this so disordered his countenance, that he found himself constrained, even though he had not before intended it, to tell *Damna*, that the terrible Noise of this Beast, whatever he was, was the Cause of all his disturbance. I imagine, said the King, that the body of the Beast which I hear bellow so dreadfully, must be proportionable to the sound of his voice; and that being so, 'tis little better than Madness for us to tarry any longer in these woods. Is this all that troubles your Majesty? said *Damna* Nothing else, answered the Lion, and this I think sufficient. Sir, replied *Damna*, you ought not to quit your princely Habitation for this: 'Tis not for a King to be afraid of a meer Sound, but rather to fortify his Courage with so much the greater Resolution. Those Creatures that make the loudest Noise are not always the biggest nor the strongest. A Crane, as big as he is, has neither strength nor courage to encounter the smallest Hawk: And he that suffers himself to be deluded by Bulk of Body, may likely enough be deceived as the Fox was.

F A B L E VII.

The FOX *and the* HEN.

THERE WAS ONCE, CONTINUED *Damna*, a certain Fox, who eagerly Searching about for something to appease his Hunger, at length spied a Hen, that was busy scratching the Earth and picking up Worms at the Foot of a Tree. Upon the same Tree there also hung a Drum, which made a Noise every now and then, the Branches being moved by the Violence of the Wind, and beating upon it. The Fox was just going to fling himself upon the Hen, and make amends for a long Fast, when he first heard the Noise of the Drum. Oh ho, quoth he, looking up, are you there, I will be with ye by and by: that Body, whatever it be, I promise myself must certainly have more Flesh upon it than a sorry Hen; so saying, he clambered up the Tree, and in the mean while the Hen made her Escape. The greedy and famished Fox seized his Prey, and fell to work with Teeth and Claws upon it. But when he had torn off the Head of the Drum, and found there was nothing within but an empty Cavity, Air instead of Flesh and Gristles, and a meer Hollowness instead of good Guts and Garbage; fetching a deep Sigh,

Unfortunate Wretch that I am, cried he, what a delicate Morsel have I lost, only for the Shew of a large Bellyfull!

I have recited this Example, concluded he, to the end your Majesty may not be terrified with the Sound of the bellowing Noise you hear, because loud and strenuous; for there is no Certainty from that of its coming from a terrible Beast: and if you please I will go and see what Sort of Creature it is. To which the Lion consented; nevertheless, when *Damna* was gone, he repented his having sent him: For, said the Monarch to himself, I should have remembered my Father's excellent Rule, that it is a great Error in a Prince to discover his Secrets to any; but especially, that there are ten Sorts of People who are never to be entrusted with them: these are, 1. Those whom he has used ill without a Cause. 2. Those who have lost their Estates or their Honour at Court. 3. Those who have been degraded from their Employments, without any Hopes of ever being restored to them again. 4. Those that love nothing but Sedition and Disturbance. 5. Those that see their Kindred or Acquaintance in Preferments from whence themselves have been excluded. 6. Such as, having committed any Crime, have been more severely punished than others who have transgressed in the same Manner. 7. Such as have done good Service, and had been but ill rewarded for it. 8. Enemies reconciled by Constraint. 9. Those who believe the Ruin of the Prince will turn to their Advantage. 10. And lastly, those who believe themselves less obliged to their Sovereign than to his Enemy. And as these are together so numerous a Class of Persons, I hope I have not done imprudently in discovering my Secrets to *Damna*.

While the King was making these Reflections to himself, *Damna* returned, and told him, with a smiling Countenance, that the Beast which made such a Noise was no other than an Ox, that was feeding in a Meadow without any other Design than to spend his Days lazily in eating and sleeping. And, added *Damna*, if your Majesty thinks it convenient, I will so order the Matter, that he shall be glad to come and enroll himself in the Number of your Servants. The Lion was extremely pleased with *Damna's* Proposals, and made him a Sign to go and fetch the Ox into his Presence. On this, *Damna* went immediately to *Cohotorbe*, and asked him from whence he came, and what Accident had brought him into those Quarters? In answer to which, when *Cohotorbe,* had related his History at large, *Damna* said, Friend, I am very glad I have happened to see thee, for it may be in my Power to do thee a singular Service, by acquainting thee with the State of the Place thou hast accidentally wandered into. Know then, that here lives a Lion not far off, who is the King of all the Beasts of this Country, and that he is, though a terrible Enemy, yet a most kind and tender Friend to all the Beasts who put themselves under his Protection. When I first saw you here I acquainted his Majesty with it, and he has graciously desired to see thee, and given me Orders to conduct thee to his Palace. If thou wilt follow me, I promise thee the Favour of being admitted into his Service and Protection; but if thou refusest to go along with me, know that thou hast not many Days to live in this Place. So soon as the Ox heard the Word Lion pronounced, he trembled for Fear; but recovering himself a little, as *Damna* continued his Speech, he at length made Answer, If thou wilt assure me that he shall do me no Harm, I will follow him. *Damna,* on this, immediately swore to him; and *Cohotorbe's,* upon the Faith of his Oath, consented to go and wait upon the Lion. *Damna,* on this, ran before to give the King Notice of *Cohotorbe's* Coming; and our Ox arriving soon after, made a profound Reverence to the King; who received him with great Kindness, and asked him what Occasion had brought him into his Dominions? In answer to which, when the Ox had recounted to him all his Adventures, Remain here, said the Lion, with us, and live in Peace; for I permit all my Subjects to live within my Dominions, in Repose and Tranquility. The Ox having returned his Majesty Thanks for his kind Reception, promised to serve him with a real Fidelity; and at length insinuated himself in such a Manner into the Lion's Favour, that he gained his Majesty's Confidence, and became his most intimate Favourite.

This, however, was Matter of great Affliction to poor *Damna,* who, when he saw that *Cohotorbe* was in greater Esteem at Court than himself, and that he was the only Depository of the King's Secrets, it wrought in him so desperate a Jealousy, that he could not rest, but was ready to hang himself for Vexation. In the Fulness of his Heart he slew to make his moan to *Kalila.* Oh my dear Wife, said he, I have taken a World of Care and Pains to gain the King's

Favour, and all to no Purpose: I brought, you may remember, into his Presence the Object that occasioned all his Disturbances, and that very Ox is now become the sole Cause of my Disquiet. To which *Kalila* answered, Spouse, you ought not to complain of what you have done, or at least you have nobody to blame but yourself. You should have considered that this might prove the Consequence when you undertook this Enterprize, for you are now just in the Condition of the Dervise who left his Habitation.

F A B L E VIII.

A Dervise *that left his Habitation.*

A certain King once presented a Dervise, who was a great Favourite with him, with a very rich Habit; of which a cunning Thief in the Neighbourhood having Notice, made use of the following Stratagem to cheat him of it: He went with a down-cast Look and demure Countenance, to the Dervise in his Habitation, and pretended an earnest Desire to serve him, and that the utmost of his Ambition was to attend on him, as his Master and great Example in Holiness, as long as he lived. The Dervise, overjoyed that he had got a Novice who seemed to be so piously inclined, most willingly received him; but the Thief taking the first Opportunity, stole the Habit, and carried it away. The Dervise missing at once both his rich Cloths and his Novice, mistrusted the Business; and so leaving his Habitation resolved to go to the City in search of the Robber. As he travelled upon the Road he met with two Rams that were very furiously encountering one another, and inter-changed such desperate Horn-blows, that the Blood ran down on every Side. A Fox, who was a Witness of the Combat, made his own Advantage of it and licked up the Blood: But at length, as he was licking, he received such a terrible Blow over the Head from one of the Rams that he died upon the Spot.

The Dervise stopped a good while to behold, and moralize upon this Accident, and in short stayed so long, that when he came to the City, the Gates were shut. A good-natur'd Woman, however, that lived in the City, looking out at a Window, and perceiving he wanted a Lodging, called to him, and offered him the Conveniency of her House. The Dervise was honest himself, and therefore suspecting no Harm of others, very readily accepted her Kindness, went into the House, and as soon as he was entered, thrust himself into a Corner to say his usual Prayers. This Woman, as the Devil would have it, was a Bawd, and kept a Bevy of pretty Girls, whose Favours she sold to the young Gentry of the Place. Now among these Girls there was one who was violently beloved by a young Gentleman, and of whom he was so jealous, that he would admit no body else to come near her; which they, who were enamoured of her as well as himself, took so ill, that they persuaded the young Girl to rid herself of his Company. And the Girl, who feared him more than she loved him, listened to the Persuasions of her other Lovers, made her jealous Tyrant drunk, and the same Night blew a poisonous Powder up his Nostrils: This Powder, however, as Mischief often rebounds on those who occasion it, forcing the young Man to sneeze, the Strength of the Sternutation blew a Part of it into the Courtezan's Mouth; and she not being able to prevent it going down her Throat, felt the Effects of her own Poison, and died the same Hour. The poor Dervise, who was a trembling Witness to all this, was astonished at the monstrous Wickedness of the World, and thought the Night extremely long.

As soon a Day came, he made haste to leave for dangerous a Place, and took a Lodging at a Shoemaker's House, who received him with open Arms; the same Evening, however, the Host being invited to a Feast from which it was impossible for him to absent himself, recommended to his Family the Care and good Usage of his Guest.

Now this Shoemaker's Wife had a Gallant, whom she was extremely fond of; he was handsome, well made, a Man of some Wit, and good-humoured; this loving Couple met frequently together by means of a certain old Surgeon's Wife, who was so cunning a Sollicitress of Lechery, that she could have reconciled Fire and Water into an amorous Conjunction, and had her Tongue so well hung, and was so perfect in the Art of wheedling, that she would have made you believe a Stone was made of Wax. Whenever the Shoemaker's Wife knew her Husband was safe abroad, she made use of this Mistress *Go-between*, to give Notice to her Paramour of his Absence; and now believing she had an excellent Opportunity, sent her away forthwith to tell her Gallant the good News. Away comes he upon the first Intimation; but by what ill Luck I know not, as he was knocking at the Door, the Shoemaker arrived, and finding the Man, whom he already suspected to be the Grafter of his Forehead, had had such good Intelligence, in he went, and without saying a Word, beat his Wife, tied her to a Post, and so went to Bed.

While the moody Cuckold, who had tired his Arms with bestowing his Strap upon his Wife, was fast asleep, and dreaming, I warrant, of Rams, Stags, Oxen and other horned Beasts, in comes the pious *Go-between*, the Surgeon's Wife, and not knowing any thing of what had happened, and having found out the Shoemaker's Wife in the Dark, 'Slife, Sister, says she, why do you let the young Man stay so long at the Door? For Shame, go and fetch him in. To whom the disappointed Bond-woman answered, with a deep Sigh, and a low Voice; I believe says she, some malicious Demon, or other, sent my Husband back from Supper; for home he came in such a Rage, that not satisfied with almost breaking my Bones, he has here tied me to a Post. Now, if you would do a charitable Act, unbind me, and stand in my Place a Moment, while I go and beg Pardon of my dear Friend, for having made him stay so long; which done, I will immediately come back and be tied as I was.

The Surgeon's Wife, moved with Compassion, and being a hearty Well-wisher to the Sweets of Whoring, made no Scruple to put herself in the Room of her distressed Neighbour, who immediately went to keep her Word with her Gallant. And the Dervise, who had heard all this Discourse, now no longer accused the Shoemaker of Cruelty.

In the mean time, however, as Luck would have it, the Shoemaker waked, and called to his Wife; but the Surgeon's Mate, fearing to be known by her Voice, made no Answer, this put the Shoemaker into such a Fury, that he leapt out of the Bed, took a Knife in his Hand, and at one Slash cut off, as he thought his Wife's Nose, and holding it in his Hand, here, said he, here is a Present for you to send your Wagtail in a Corner.

The poor Surgeon's Wife, though in the utmost Agony, durst not so much as sigh for Fear; however, quoth she to herself, this is very hard Luck, for me to suffer what the Shoemaker's Wife deserves, while she his toying and dallying in the Arms of her Lover.

The Shoemaker's Wife on her Return, you may easily imagine, was very much surprised to find her faithful Help-mate without a Nose; begged a thousand hearty Pardons, unbound her, and tied herself in her Place, while the Surgeon's Mate returned home, carrying her Nose in her Hand.

Some Hours after this, when she thought her Husband might hear her, with her Hands lifted up to Heaven, Most powerful Deity, cried she who knowest the Secrets of all Hearts, thou knowest that my Husband has abused me without a Cause, let him see that I am a Woman of Reputation, by removing from my Face the Deformity with which his Cruelty has defaced it, and restoring me my Nose as it was before. The Shoemaker hearing those Words, Vile Strumpet, cried he, what wicked Prayer art thou making? Knowest thou not that the Prayers of Harlots never reach the Throne of Heaven? Prayers that would be heard must issue from a clean Heart, and undefiled Lips. Villainous and inhuman Tyrant, cried his Wife, rise and admire the Puissance of the Deity, and the Excess of his Goodness, who knowing my Innocence of the Crime for which thou accusest me, is pleased to demonstrate my Chastity, by restoring me my Nose, to the End I may not be looked upon as a Woman of Dishonour in the World. The Shoemaker, believing such a Miracle impossible, rises, lights a Candle, comes to his Wife, and finding upon her Face no Mark at all of the cruel Fact which he thought he had committed, confessed the Injury he had done her to suspect her, begged her Pardon, and by a thousand Caresses strove to make her forget his Cruelty.

The Surgeon's Wife, on the other hand, who was gone home to her Lodging, as you may well believe, in great Affliction, crept softly into Bed to her Husband, who when he waked, asked her for his Case of Instruments, that he might go and dress of Person he had promised to be with before Day. His Wife was a long time seeking what her Husband demanded, and when she saw him quite out of Patience, gave him a single Razor, which put him into such a Fury that he flung it at her Head, calling her a thousand Jades and Baggages. 'Twas hardly Day when this happened, which favoured the noseless Lady's Design. Presently therefore she flung herself upon the Ground, and filled the Air with loud Shrieks of Murder, Murder, which fetched all her Neighbours in an Instant about her; who seeing her all bloody, and without a Nose, began to cry out Shame upon the Surgeon, who was so astonished, that he knew not what to say, nor which Way to look. He knew not whether it were best for him to deny our confess the Fact: However, when Morning was come, they hurried the Surgeon away before the Magistrate, and demanded Justice on him for his Barbarity. As Fortune would have it, however, the Dervise also went along with the Rabble, and heard the Case stated.

After the Witnesses were heard, Well, said the Judge to the Surgeon, what have you to say for yourself? What was the Reason that you abused your Wife in this horrid Manner? To which when the Surgeon, seized with Astonishment, stood mute, not knowing what to answer, the Judge without farther Examination was going to condemn him to Death.

On this the Dervise, who had with Horror and Amazement seen this and the other Adventures of his Journey, and was as it were possessed with the Remembrance of them to such a Degree, that he could not forbear continually repeating them in his Mind, cried out, Hold, O Judge! suspend your Judgment and take care what Sentence you pronounce; 'tis neither the Thief that stole my Garments, nor the Rams that killed the Fox, nor the Harlot that poisoned her Lover, nor, lastly, the Shoemaker that cut off the Surgeon's Wife's Nose, but every one of the Sufferers who have drawn upon themselves all these Misfortunes. Then the Judge leaving the Surgeon, and addressing himself to the Dervise, demanded the Interpretation of his Riddle.

The Dervise, in answer, gave him a full Account of all that

he had seen; and moralizing on the whole, Sir, said, he, had I not taken the rich Garment out of Ambition, the Thief had never robbed me; had not the Fox thrown himself between the Rams out of Greediness, he had not been killed: had not the Courtezan gone about to poison the young Gentleman, she had not perished herself; and had not the Surgeon's Wife favoured the Adultery of the Shoemaker's, she had never lost her Nose. And from the whole this short Lesson is to be learned, that they who commit Evil cannot hope for Good.

I have made use of this Fable, said *Kalila* to her Spouse, to shew you that you have brought these Troubles upon your own Head. 'Tis true, said *Damna*, that I am the Cause of them; this I am too sensible of, but what I desire of you is, to prescribe me the Remedy. I told you from the Beginning, replied *Kalila,* that for my part I would never meddle with your Affairs, and now don't intend to trouble myself with the Cure of your Disturbances. Mind your own Business yourself, and consider what Course you have to take, and take it; for as to me, I have Plagues enough of my own, without making myself unhappy about the Misfortunes that your own Follies have brought upon you. Well then, replied *Damna,* what I shall do is this, I will use all my Endeavours to ruin this Ox which occasions me all my Misery, and shall be contented if I but find I have as much Wit as the Sparrow that revenged himself upon the Hawk. *Kalila* upon this desired him to recite that Fable, and *Damna* gave it her in the following Manner.

F A B L E IX.

The SPARROW *and the* SPARROW-HAWK.

Two Sparrows had once built their Nests under the same Hovel, where they had also laid up some small Provision for their young ones; but a Sparrow-Hawk, who had built his Nest upon the Top of a Mountain, at the Foot of which this Hovel stood, came continually to watch at what time their Eggs would be hatched; and when they were, immediately eat up the young Sparrows. This was a most sensible Affliction to both the Parents. However, they had afterwards another Brood, which they hid so among the Thatch of the Hovel, that the Hawk was never able to find them; these therefore they bred up so well, and in so much Safety, that they had both of them the Pleasure to see them ready to fly. The Father and the Mother, by their continual chirping testified for a long time their Joy for such a Happiness; but all of a sudden, as the young ones began to be fledged, they fell into a profound Melancholy, which was caused through Extremity of Fear lest for Sparrow-Hawk should devour these young ones as he had done the others, as soon as they found their Way out of the Nest. The eldest of these young Sparrows one Day perceiving this, desired to know of the Father the Reason of his Affliction, which the Farther having discovered to him, he made Answer, that instead of breaking his Heart with Sorrow, it much better became him to seek out some Way, if possible, to remove so dangerous a Neighbour. All the Sparrows approved this Advice of the young one; and while the Mother flew to get Food, the Father went another Way in search of some Cure for his Sorrows. After he had flown about for some time, said he to himself, I know not, alas! what it is I am seeking. Whither shall I fly? and to whom shall I discover my Troubles? at length he resolved, not knowing what Course to take, to address himself to the first Creature he met, and to consult him about his Business. This first Creature chanced to be a Salamander, whose extraordinary Shape at first affrighted him: However, the Sparrow would not alter his Resolution, but accosted and saluted him. The Salamander, who was very civil, gave him an obliging Reception; and looking upon him with a fixed Eye, Friend, said he, I discover much Trouble in thy countenance; if it proceed from Weariness, sit down and rest thyself; if from any other Cause, let me know it, and if it be in my Power to serve thee, command me. With that the Sparrow told his Misfortunes in such moving Language as raised Compassion in the Salamander. Well, said he be of Courage, let not these Troubles any more perplex thee, I'll deliver thee from this wicked Neighbour this very Night; only shew me his Nest, and then go peaceably to roost with thy young Ones; this the Sparrow accordingly punctually did, and returned the Salamander many Thanks for being so much concerned for his Misfortunes. No sooner was the Night come, but the Salamander, determined to make good his Promise, collected together a Number of his Fellows, and away they went in a Body, with every one a Bit of lighted Sulphur in their Mouths to the Sparrow-Hawk's Nest, who, not dreaming of any such thing, was surprised by the Salamanders, who threw the Sulphur into the Nest, and burnt the old Hawk, with all the young Ones.

This Fable teaches you, that whoever has a Design to ruin his Enemy, may possibly bring it about let him be never so weak. But consider, Spouse, replied *Kalila, Cohotorbe* is the King's chief Favourite, and it will be a difficult thing, believe me, to ruin him: where prudent Princes have once placed their Confidence they seldom withdraw it because of bare Report; and I presume you will not be able to use any other Means on this Occasion. I will take care, however replied *Damna*, of this, at least, that it shall be represented to the Lion, that one of the six great Things which caused the Ruin of Kingdoms, and which is indeed the principal, is to neglect and contemn Men of Wit and Courage. That indeed, replied *Kalila*, is one very great one; but what, I pray, are the other five? The second, continued *Damna*, is not to punish the Seditious; the third is to be too much given to Woman, to Play and Divertisements; the fourth, the Accidents attending a Pestilence, a Famine, or an Earthquake; the fifth is being too rash and violent; and the sixth is, the preferring War before Peace. You are wise and prudent, Spouse, replied *Kalila*, but let me, tho'more simple, advice thee in this Matter: Be not the Carver of your own Revenge; but consider that whoever meditates Mischief, commonly brings it at last upon his own Head. On the other Side, he that studies his Neighbour's Welfare, prospers in every thing he undertakes, as you may see by the ensuing Fable.

FABLE X.

The KING *who from a* SAVAGE TYRANT *became benign and just.*

THERE was once in the eastern Part of *Egypt* a King whose Reign had long been a Course of savage Tyranny; long had he ruined the Rich, and distressed the Poor; so that all his Subjects, Day and Night, implored of Heaven to be delivered from him. One Day, as he returned from hunting, after he had summoned his People together: Unhappy Subjects, says he to them, my Conduct has been long unjustifiable in regard to you: But that Tyranny, with which I have governed hithto, is at an end, and I assure you from henseforward you shall live in Peace and at Ease, and no body shall dare to oppress you. The People were extremely overjoyed at this good News, and forbore praying against the King.

In a word, this Prince made from this time such an Alteration in his Conduct, that he acquired the Title of the Just, and every one began to bless the Felicity of his Reign. One Day, when his Subjects were thus settled in Happiness, one of his Favourites presuming to ask him the Reason of so sudden and so remarkable a Change, the King gave him this Answer: As I rode a hunting the other Day, said he, I saw a

Series of Accidents which threw me into a Turn of Mind that has produced this happy Change; which, believe me, cannot give my People more real Satisfaction than it does myself. The Things that made this Change in me were these; I saw a Dog in pursuit of a Fox, who after he had over-taken him, bit off the lower Part of his Leg; however, the Fox, lame as he was, made a shift to escape and get into a Hole, and the Dog, not able to get him out, left him there: Hardly had he gone, however, a hundred Paces, when a Man threw a great Stone at him and cracked his Skull; at the same Instant the Man ran in the Way of a Horse, that trod upon his Foot and lamed him forever; and soon after, the Horse's Foot struck so fast between two Stones, that he broke his Ancle-bone in striving to get it out. On seeing these sudden Misfortunes befal those who had engaged in doing ill to others, I could not help saying to myself, Men are used as they use others: Whoever does that which he ought not to do, receives what he is not willing to receive.

This Example shews you, my dear Spouse, that they who do Mischief to others, are generally punished themselves for it, when they least expect it: Believe me, if you attempt to ruin *Cohotorbe*, you will repent of it; he is stronger than you, and has more Friends. No matter for that, dear Spouse, replied *Damna*, Wit is always beyond Strength, as the following Fable will convince you.

F A B L E XI.

A Raven, *a* Fox, *and a* Serpent.

A Raven had once built her Nest for many Seasons together in a convenient Cleft of a Mountain, but however pleasing the Place was to her, she had always Reason enough to resolve to lay there no more; for every time she hatched, a Serpent came and devoured her young Ones. This Raven complaining to a Fox that was one of her Friends, said to him, pray tell me, what would you advise me to do to be rid of this Serpent? What do you think to do? answered the Fox. Why, my present Intent is, replied the Raven, to go and pect out his Eyes when he is asleep, that so he may no longer find the way to my Nest. The Fox disapproved this Design, and told the Raven, that it became a prudent Person to manage his Revenge in such a Manner, that no Mischief might befal himself in taking it: Never run yourself says he, into the Misfortune that once befel the Crane, of which I will tell you the Fable.

F A B L E XII.

The CRANE *and the* CRAY-FISH.

A Crane had once settled her Habitation by the Side of a broad and deep Lake, and lived upon such Fish as she could catch in it: these she got in Plenty enough, for many Years; but at length being became old and feeble, she could fish no longer. In this afflicting Circumstance she began to reflect, with Sorrow, on the Carelessness of her past Years; I did ill, said she to herself, in not making in my Youth necessary Provision to support me in my old Age; but, as it is, I must now make the best of a bad Market, and use Cunning to get a Livelihood as I can: With this Resolution she placed herself by the Water-side, and began to sigh and look mighty melancholy. A Cray-fish, perceiving her at a Distance, accosted her, and asked her why she appeared so sad? Alas, said she, how can I otherwise chuse but grieve, seeing my daily Nourishment is like to be taken from me? For I just now heard this Talk between two Fishermen passing this Way: said the one to the other, Here is great Store of Fish, what think you of clearing this Pond; to whom his Companion answered, No ————— there is more in such a Lake: Let us go thither first, and then come hither the Day afterwards. This they will certainly perform, and then, added the Crane, I must soon prepare for Death.

The Cray-fish on this, went to the Fish and told them what she had heard: Upon which the poor Fish in great Perplexity swam immediately to the Crane, and addressing themselves to her, told her what they had heard, and added, We are now in so great a Consternation, that we are come to desire your Protection. Though you are our Enemy, yet the Wise tell us, that they who make their Enemy their Sanctuary, may be assured of being well received: You know full well that we are your daily Food; and if we are destroyed, you, who are now too old to travel in search of Food, must also perish: we pray you, therefore, for your own Sake, as well as ours, to consider and tell us what you think is the best Course for us to take. To which the Crane replied, that which you acquaint me with, I heard myself from the Mouths of the Fishermen; we have no Power sufficient to withstand them; nor do I know any other way to secure you, but this: It will be many Months before they can clear the other Pond they are to go about first; and, in the mean time, I can at times, and as my Strength will permit me, remove you one after another into a little Pond here hard by, where there is very good Water, and where the Fishermen can never catch you, by reason of the extraordinary Depth. The Fish approved this Counsel, and desired the Crane to carry them one by one into this Pond. Nor did she fail to fish up three or four every Morning, but she carried them no farther than to the Top of a small Hill, where she eat them: and thus she feasted herself for a while.

But one Day, the Cray-fish, having a desire to see this delicate Pond, made known her Curiosity to the Crane, who, bethinking herself that the Cray-fish was her most mortal Enemy, resolved to get rid of her at once, and murder her as she had done the rest; With this Design she flung the Cray-fish upon her Neck, and flew towards the Hill. But when they came near the Place, the Cray-fish, spying at a distance the small Bones of her slaughtered Companions, mistrusted the Crane's Intention, and laying hold of a fair Opportunity got her Neck in her Claw, and grasped it so hard, that she fairly saved herself, and strangled the Crane.

This example, says the Fox, shews you, that crafty, tricking People often become Victims to their own Cunning.

The Raven, returning Thanks to the Fox for his good Advice, said, I shall not by any means neglect you wholesome Instructions; but what shall I do? Why, replied the Fox, You must snatch up something that belongs to some stout Man or other, and let him see what you do, to the end he may follow you. Which that he may easily do, do you fly slowly; and when you are just over the Serpent's Hole, let fall the Thing that you hold in your Beak or Talons, whatever it be, for then the Person that follows you, seeing the Serpent come forth, will not fail to knock him on the Head. The Raven did as the Fox advised him, and by that Means was delivered from the Serpent.

What cannot be done by Strength, said *Damna,* is to be performed by Policy. It is very true, replied *Kalila;* but the Mischief here is, that the Ox has more Policy then you. He will, by his Prudence, frustrate all your Projects, and before you can pluck one Hair from his Tail, will flea off your Skin. I know not whether you have ever heard of the Fable of the Rabbet, the Fox, and the Wolf; if not, I will tell it to you, that you may make your Advantage of it in the present Case.

F A B L E XIII.

The RABBET, *the* FOX, *and the* WOLF.

A Hungry Wolf once spied a Rabbet feeding at the Foot of a Tree, and was soon preparing to seize him. The Rabbet perceiving him, would have saved his Life by Flight, but the Wolf threw himself in his Way, and stopped his Escape: so that seeing himself in the Power of the Wolf, submissive and prostrate at his Feet, he gave him all the good Words he could think of. I know, said he, that the King of all Creatures wants a Supply to appease his Hunger, and that he is now ranging the Fields in search of Food; but I am but an insignificant Morsel for his Royal Stomach; therefore let him be pleased to take my Information. About a Furlong from hence lives a Fox that is fat and plump, and whose Flesh is as white as a Capon's: Such a Prey will do your Majesty's Business. If you please I will go and give him a Visit, and engage him to come forth out of his Hole: Then, if he prove to your Liking, you may devour him: if not, it will be my Glory that I had the Honour of dying not in vain, but being a small Breakfast for your Majesty.

Thus over-persuaded, the Wolf gave the Rabbet leave to seek out the Fox, and followed him at the Heels. The

Rabbet left the Wolf at the Entrance of the Hole, and crept in himself, overjoyed that he had such an Opportunity to revenge himself on the Fox, from whom he had received an Affront which he had for a long time pretended to have forgot. He made him a low Congee, and gave him great Protestations of his Friendship. On the other Side, the Fox was no less obliging in his Answers to the Rabbet's Civilities, and asked him what good Wind had blown him thither. Only the great Desire I had to see your Worship, replied the Rabbet, and there is one of my Relations at the Door, who is no less ambitious to kiss your Hands, but he dares not enter without your Permission. The Fox, on this, mistrusting there was something more than ordinary in all this Civility, said to himself, I shall find the Bottom of all this presently, and then, if it proves as I suspect, I will take care to pay this pretended Friend of mine in his own Coin. However, not seeming to take any Notice of what he suspected, Sir, said he to the Rabbet, your Friend shall be most welcome, does me too much honour ————— but, added he, I must interest you to let me put my Chamber in a little better Order to receive him. The Rabbet too much persuaded of the good Success of his Enterprize; Puh, puh, said he, my Relation is one that never stands upon Ceremonies, and so went out to give the Wolf Notice that the Fox was fallen into the Snare. The Wolf thought he had the Fox fast already, and the Rabbet believed himself quite out of danger, as having done the Wolf such a piece of good service. But the Fox was too sharp-sighted to be thus trapanned out of his Life. He had, at the Entrance of his Hole, a very deep Trench, which he had digged on purpose to guard him against Surprises of this Nature. Presently therefore he took away the Planks, which he had laid for the Convenience of those that came to visit him, covered the Trench with a little Earth and Straw, and set open a back Door in case of Necessity; and having thus prepared all things, he desired the Rabbet and his Friend to walk in. But instead of the Success of their Plot, the two Visiters found themselves, before they expected it, in the Bottom of a very deep Pit, and the Wolf, imagining that the Rabbet had a hand in the Contrivance, in the Heat of his Fury tore him to Pieces.

By this you see, that Finesse and Policy signify nothing, where you have Persons of Wit and Prudence to deal with.

'Tis very true, said *Damna*, but the Ox is now proud of his Preferment, and thoughtless of Danger, at least from me; for he has not the least Suspicion of my Hatred. A Rabbet, wiser than that you have been speaking of, once undertook the Ruin of a Lion, and you shall see how he brought it about.

F A B L E XIV.

The LION and the RABBET.

In the Neighbourhood of *Mianstol** there was a very delightful Meadow, where several wild Beasts had taken up their Habitiations, by reason of the Pleasantness of the Place. Among those Creatures there was a furious Lion, who disturbed the Peace of all the rest, with his continual Murders. In order to remedy this dreadful Evil, one Day they met all together, went to wait upon the Lion, and laid their Case before him, that they were his Subjects, and by consequence, that it no way became him to make, every Day, such dreadful Slaughters among them, of whole Families together. You seek after us, added they, to rule over us, but though we are proud of a King of so much Valour, yet in Fear we avoid you; would you live peaceably with us, and enjoy your Quiet, by letting us alone, we would bring you every Morning Sufficient, and delicate Food, nor should you ever want to crown your Meals with a Flasket of tame and wild Fowl, and you should, yourself, never be put to the

---

* *Mianstol* is a large Tract of Country on the Banks of the *Ganges,* uninhabited, except by a great Number of wild Beasts.

Toil of Hunting. The Lion readily accepted this Proposal, and the Beasts cast Lots every Morning, and he upon whom the Lot fell was appointed to hunt for the Lion.

One Day the Lot fell upon a Rabbet, who seeing he could not avoid it, after he had summoned all the Beasts together, said to them, you see how miserable a Life 'tis we lead here, either we must be eaten ourselves, or spend our Labour to feed a churlish Master. Now hear what I have to propose; do you but stand by me, and I will certainly deliver you from this cruel Tyrant that reigns over us. To this they all unanimously answered, that they would do their utmost: Upon this the Rabbet said in his Hold till the Hour of Dinner was past, and made no Provision for the Lion. By this Time the Lion's Anger augmented with his Appetite; he lashed the Ground with his Tail, and at length perceiving the Rabbet, whence come you, said he, and what are my Subjects doing? Do they suppose, I accepted their Proposal, and spared their Lives, to be kept without Victuals by their Idleness; be assured, if I wait much longer, they shall, some of them, severly pay for it. May it please your Majesty to hear me, answered the Rabbet, bowing to him with a profound Respect; your Subjects, sacred Sir, have not been wanting in their Duty; they sent me hither to bring your Majesty your accustomed Provision; but I met a Lion by the Way, who took it from me. I told him, when he seized it, that it was for the King: To which he most insolently answered, that there was no other King in this Country but himself. Struck dumb with this monstrous Behaviour, I left him, and ran to inform your Majesty of this hainous Piece of Insolence. The Lion, on this, furiously turning about his burning Eyes, cried out, Who is this audacious Usurper that dares to lay his Paw upon my Food, which my Subjects had laboured to provide for me? Can't thou show me where the audacious Traitor lives? Yes, Sir, replied the Rabbet, if you will be pleased to follow me. The Lion breathing Revenge and Destruction, followed the wily Rabbet; and when they came to a Well that was full of clear Water, Sir, said the Rabbet, your Enemy lives in this Well, I dare not show him you, but only be pleased to look in yourself, and you will see him: Have a care, however, that you are not first assailed. With that the Lion went stalking to the Well, and seeing the Reflection of his own Image, which he took to be another Lion in the Water, that had devoured his Food, enflamed with Anger he flung himself into the Well to encounter this mortal Foe, and there was drowned himself. This Fable shows you, that a strong Person may be destroyed by one that is much weaker, when he is not mistrusted. Well, well, said *Kalila,* if you can ruin the Ox without doing the Lion any Harm, go on and prosper; if not, I advise you to give over your Enterprise; For it does not become a Subject, for his own private Interest and Repose, to suffer any Mischief to befal his Prince.

Here the Confabulation between *Damna* and *Kalila* ended, and *Damna* having taken leave of his Wife, absented himself for some Time from the Lion's Court. Afterwards he returned, and affecting an Air of Sadness before his Majesty, Honest *Damna,* said to the King to him, whence comest thou? Where hast thou been this long Time? Is there any News abroad? Yes, Sir, Answered *Damna* with a deep Sigh, there is News indeed: Such News as I dread to speak, yet such as your Majesty ought to hear. On this the King, starting for Fear, cried out, What is it? I beg your Majesty, replied *Damna,* since you will hear it, that you will be pleased to grant me a private Audience. Affairs of Importance ought never to be delayed, replied the King; and so commanding the Room to be immediately cleared, ordered *Damna* to speak what he had to say. 'Tis requisite, said that wily Minister, that the Bearer of ill News should have the address to give it an Allay; and it is also most necessary, that he to whom it is reported, should be able to judge, whether the Person that makes the Report be worthy to be credited, or whether he speak falsely and for the Sake of his own Interest; and if he be worthy to be believed, he ought to be entirely confided in, when his Discourse may be advantageous to the Public, or, what is yet of greater Consequence, to the Sovereign himself. On this, the Lion interrupting him, thou know'st, said he, that I have experienced thy Fidelity, and therefore speak boldly what thou hast to say. The Purity of my Intentions, continued *Damna,* have made me to assume this Boldness, and I am more than happy to be known to your Majesty. I question not thy Zeal, said the Lion; but pr'ythee come to this News, which it so much concerns me to know.

When *Damna* perceived the good Success of his Flatteries, and that the King had a Confidence in him, he thus began his Discourse. Sir, said he, I am sorry to relate it, but my excellently esteemed Friend, and your Majesty's great Favourite, *Cohortorbe,* has daily Conferences with the Grandees and Chieftains of your Army, and I know that in them he improves every Circumstance, as much as lies in his Power, to your Majesty's Prejudice; which makes me believe he has some Design upon your sacred Person. I grieve to tell this, and am not less astonished than angry, when I reflect that he should so ungratefully abuse your Favours, and the particular Friendship with which you are pleased to honour him. *Damna,* cried the Lion, take care what thou say'st; thou art accusing one of whom I have a settled good opinion: But if this be true, what Course is to be taken? Sir, replied *Damna,* there are two Sorts of People in the World, the one sage and prudent, the other rash and inconsiderate. The one are always at a loss, when any Accident befals them; the other always foresees things, and therefore nothing moves them, whatever happens. We ought, Sir, to imitate their Prudence, and secure overselves from Danger, so soon as we have the least Notice or Intimation of it. There are also, beside these, yet another Sort of People, who, I have observed, never truly foresee Danger; but, however, know how to take their proper Course when it presents itself: And these three Characters put me in mind of the Fable of the three Fish, which I would tell your Majesty, did I not fear it would offend your Patience. The Lion, on this, commanded *Damna* to let him hear it out; so *Damna* thus proceeded.

F A B L E XV.

The two FISHERMEN *and the three* FISH.

THERE was once in your Majesty's Dominions a certain Pond, the Water of which was very clear, and emptied itself into a neighbouring River. This Pond was in a quiet Place; it was remote from the Highway, and there were in it three Fish; the one of which was prudent, the second had but little Wit, and the third was a mere Fool. One Day, by chance, two Fishermen, in their Walks, perceiving this Pond, made up to it, and no sooner observed these three Fish which were large and fat, but they went and fetched their Nets to take them. The Fish suspecting, by what they saw of the Fishermen, that they intended no less than their destruction, began to be in a World of Terror. The prudent Fish immediately resolved what Course to take: He threw himself out of the Pond, through the little Channel that opened into the River, and so made his Escape. The next Morning the two Fishermen returned; they made it their first Business to stop all the Passages, to prevent the Fish from getting out, and were making Preparations for taking them. The half-witted Fish now heartily repented that he had not followed his Companion; at length, however, he bethought himself of a Stratagem; he appeared upon the Surface of the Water with his Belly upward, and feigned to be dead. The Fishermen also having taken him up, thought him really what he counterfeited to be, so threw him again into the Water. And the last, which was the foolish Fish, seeing himself pressed by the Fishermen, sunk down to Bottom of the Pond, shifted up and down from Place to Place, but could not avoid, at last, falling into their Hands, and was that Day made Part of a public Entertainment.

This Example, continued *Damna*, shews your Majesty, that you ought to prevent *Cohotorbe* from doing the Mischief he intends, by making yourself Master of his Life, before he have yours at his Command. What you say is very agreeable to Reason, said the King, but I cannot yet believe that *Cohotorbe*, upon whom I have heaped so many Favours, should be so perfidious as you represent him. Why, it is most true, replied *Damna*, that he never received any thing but Kindness from your Majesty, but *what is bred in the Bone will never out of the Flesh; neither can any thing come out of a Vessel but what is put into it.* Of which the following Fable is a sufficient Proof.

F A B L E XVI.

The SCORPION *and the* TORTOISE.

A Tortoise and Scorpion had once contracted a great
Intimacy, and bound themselves in such a Tie of
Friendship, that the one could not live without the other.
These inseparable Companions, one Day, finding
themselves obliged to change their Habitation, travelled
together, but in their Way meeting with a large deep River,
the Scorpion, making a Stop, said to the Tortoise, My dear
Friend, you are well provided for what we see before us, but
how shall I get over this Water? Never trouble yourself, my
dear Friend, for that, replied the Tortoise, I will carry you
upon my Back secure from all danger. The Scorpion on
this, without Hesitation, got upon the Back of the Tortoise,
who immediately took Water and began to swim. But he was
hardly get half was across the River, when he heard a
terrible Rumbling upon his Back, which made him ask the
Scorpion what he was doing? Doing! replied the Scorpion,
why I am whetting my Sting, to try whether I can bore this
horny Cuirass of yours that covers your Flesh like a Shield
from all Injuries. Oh ingrateful Wretch, cried the Tortoise,
wouldst thou, at a time when I am giving thee such a

Demonstration of my Friendship, wouldst thou at such a time, pierce with thy venonmous Sting the Defence that Nature has given me, and take away my Life?

It is well, however, I have it in my Power, both to save myself and reward thee as thou deservest; so saying, he sunk his Back to some Depth under Water, threw off the Scorpion, and left him to pay his Life, the just Forfeit of his monstrous Ingratitude, Had he not destroyed his ungrateful Favourite, in this Manner, Royal Sir, continued *Damna*, his own Life had paid for it; and it is good, and most just general Rule, that the Wicked are never to be favoured. You urge me too hard upon this Subject, said the Lion and I cannot but think that were *Cohotorbe* capable of so much Perfidiousness, he would certainly have shewn his malicious Intentions before. Never trust to that, replied *Damna*, he carries on his Design with more Prudence. He will not, Royal Sir, attack your Majesty's Person openly and publicly himself; no, but he will cajole your whole Court, and delude them into his Interests, and then take his own Time to destroy your sacred Person, and openly avowing his Guilt, perhaps, set himself up for King in your Place. Just Heaven keep me from seeing such a Day! Providence defend me from such Masters! You say something indeed now, said the Lion, interrupting him, but now I know him guilty, how shall we find a fair Pretence to be rid of him? Let me alone for that, replied *Damna*, a faithless Subject must be punished.

These Amusements of the subtle Fox made such an Impression in the Mind of the King, that he at length told *Damna* he was come to a Resolution to admit *Cohotorbe* no more into his Presence, but to banish him altogether from his Court, after he had upbraided him with his Ingratitude, and let him know the Reason of his Fall. This Resolution, however, was far enough from being pleasing to *Damna*; a guilty Conscience never can have Rest. He feared that if the King once came to talk with *Cohotorbe*, all his Villiany would be discovered. On this, said he to the Lion, Sir, if I may continue my Boldness of speaking to your Majesty, I have heard from Persons of Understanding that a Prince ought never to inflict public Punishment upon Faults committed in secret; nor secretly to chastise public Crimes: Therefore, seeing *Cohotorbe* is a secret Transgressor, he must be privately punished. No, replied the Lion, it is a great Piece of Injustice to punish any one before he be told the Reason of his Punishment. To satisfy yourself of his Guilt, replied *Damna*, it will be sufficient that once for all you make him sensible of your Displeasure, and give him a cold Reception: His Conscience will upbraid him with his Perfidiousness at the same Instant, and he will no longer doubt but that you are preparing for him his due Reward: And you will perceive him accordingly disturbed and agitated in his Mind, which will be an evident Proof of the Truth of my Suspicions. If it prove so, replied the Lion, I shall be soon convinced of his Treason.

Damna now seeing the King prepared to his Heart's Desire, went to *Cohotorbe*, and made him a low Bow. To whom, the Ox, after many Caresses, said, my good old Friend, what is the Reason that you come to see me no oftner? Is it because you think me no longer one of your Friends? Though I have been absent for some time, replied *Damna*; yet, believe me, I have still preserved you in my Thoughts. But why, replied the Ox, did you retire from the Court? For this plain Reason, replied *Damna*, because I love my Liberty; and when we are in the King's Presence, we tremble for Fear, as always being under Restraint. If I mistake you not, Friend replied *Cohotorbe*, you look as if you were not satisfied with the King, and were afraid of some Misfortune or foul Play. Indeed you have guess'd but too well the Cause of my Uneasiness, answered *Damna:* I tremble, and am as troubled as you can conceive me to be; but it is for your Sake, Friend, not for my own, that I am in this Perplexity. Poor *Cohotorbe* terribly frighted at this Answer, quaking for Fear, says to *Damna*, My dear Friend, let me know the Danger that threatens me, that, if possible, I may guard against it. To this *Damna*, with a Look of great Compassion, replied, It is but just, Friend, that you should know your Danger, nor should I act consistently with that Friendship I have ever professed to you, not to acquaint you with it: The Truth therefore is this: A Friend of mine has instructed me with a private Discourse which passed some Days ago, between the King and a great Person who has no Kindness for your Lordship. Said the King to this great Person, *I have been considering that* Cohotorbe *is now very fat and of no use to us*; *and as I must a few Days hence feast all the Lords of my Court, I think my cheapest way will be to roast this Ox alive and whole for their Entertainment.* I tremble to repeat this;

but as I knew it, I could not but inform you of it, and bring you this News, to convince you that I am your real Friend, and to assist you, as far as lies in my Power, to avoid the Danger. *Cohotorbe* was astonished at this Piece of dismal Intelligence: But by what Device, said he, shall I be able to escape this intended Cruelty of the King? Alas! good Heaven is my Witness, I never gave him the least Occasion to use me so severely. Certainly I must have some private Enemy who has falsely accused me behind my Back, and incensed him without a Cause against me. And a Prince who discards and punishes a Servant, on such Grounds, is like the Drake, who seeing the Resemblance of the Moon in the Water, thought it to be some extraordinary Fish, and, deluded with that Error, dived several Times to catch it; but mad to see that all his Effects proved vain, in a violent Rage came out of the Water, swearing never to return to that Element again: And after that, though he were never so hungry, would never dive more after any Fish, believing it to be only the Light of the Moon: But for me, unhappy that I am, Backbiters and Flatterers have so prepossessed the Lion against me, that whatever I do henceforward to please him, he will still believe that I only dissemble. I know not what to say, or how to advise in this Case, replied *Damna*, the King may see his Error, and alter his Mind; but then, on the other Side, being absolute in his Power, he may, without being bound to give any Reason for it, condemn you to Death. It is most true, replied *Cohotorbe*, that Princes often seek the Destruction of those who seem their greatest Favourites. And many, who envy the Grandeur and Ease of a Court-life, know not the dangerous Accidents that attend it. As you may learn by the ensuing Fable.

F A B L E XVII.

The FALCON *and the* HEN.

OF all the Animals I was ever acquainted with, said a Falcon once to a Hen, you are the most unmindful of Benefits, and the most ungrateful. Why, what Ingratitude, replied the Hen have you ever observed in me? Can there be a greater Piece of Ingratitude, replied the Falcon, than that which you commit in regard to Men? By Day they seek out every Nourishment to fat you; and in the Night you have a Place always ready to roost in, where they take care that your Chamber be close barred up, that nothing may trouble your Repose: Nevertheless, when they would catch you, you forget all their Goodness to you, and basely endeavour to escape their Hands; which is what I never do, I that am a wild Creature, no way obliged to them, and a Bird of Prey. Upon the meanest of their Caresses I grow tame; suffer myself to be taken, and never eat but upon their Fists. All this is very true, replied the Hen; but I find you know not the Reason of my Flight; you never saw a Falcon upon the Spit, but I have seen a thousand Hens dressed with all manner of Sauces.

I have recited this Fable to shew you, that often they who are ambitious of a Court-life, know not the Inconveniences of it. I believe, Friend, said *Damna*, that the Lion seeks your Life for no other Reason but because he is jealous of your Virtues. The Fruit-trees only, replied *Cohotorbe*, are subject to have their Branches broken; Nightingales are caged because they sing more pleasantly than other Birds; and we pluck Peacock's Feathers from their Tails, for no other Reason but because they are beautiful. Merit alone is therefore, too often, the Source and Origin of our Misfortunes. However I am not afraid of whatever Contrivances the Malice of wicked People can make to my Prejudice; but shall endeavour to submit to what I cannot prevent, and imitate the Nightingale in the following Fable.

F A B L E XVIII.

The NIGHTINGALE *and the* COUNTRYMAN.

A certain Countryman had a Rose bush in his Garden, which he made his sole Pleasure and Delight. Every Morning he went to look upon it, in the Season of its flowering, and see his Roses ready to blow. One Day as he was admiring, according to his Custom, the Beauty of the Flowers, he spied a Nightingale, perched upon one of the Branches near a very fine Flower, and plucking off the Leaves of it one after another. This put him into so great a Passion that the next Day he laid a snare for the Nightingale, in Revenge of the Wrong: in which he succeeded so well, that he took the Bird and immediately put her in a cage. The Nightingale, very melancholy to see herself in that Condition, with a mournful Voice asked the Countryman the Reason of her Slavery. To whom he replied, Knowest thou not that my whole Delight was in those Flowers, which thou wast wantonly destroying; every Leaf that thou pluckedst from that Rose was a Drop of Blood from my Heart. Alas! replied the Nightingale, you use me very severely for having cropt a few Leaves from a Rose; but expect to be used harshly in the other World, for afflicting me in this Manner; for there all People are used after the same Manner as they here use the other Animals. The Countryman, moved with these Words, gave the Nightingale her Liberty again; for which she, willing to thank him, said, Since you have had Compassion in your Nature, and have done me in this Favour, I will repay your Kindness in the Manner it deserves. Know therefore, continued she, that, at the Foot of yonder Tree, there lies buried a Pot of Gold, go and take it, and Heaven bless you with it. The Countryman digged about the Tree, and finding the Pot, astonished at the Nightingale's Sagacity in discovering it; I wonder, said he to her, that, being able to see this Pot, which was buried under Ground, you could not discover the Net that was spread for your Captivity? Know you not, replied the Nightingale, that, however sharp fighted or prudent we are, we can never escape our Destiny?

By this example you see that, when we are conscious of our own Innocence, we are wholly to resign ourselves up to our Fate. 'Tis very true replied *Damna*; the Lion, however, according to the most just Observation of the captive Nightingale in your Fable, in seeking your Destruction, cannot but incur divine Punishment; and, desirous as he is to augment his Grandeur by your Fall, I am apt to think that what once befel the Hunter will be his Destiny.

F A B L E XIX.

The HUNTER, *the* FOX, *and the* LEOPARD.

A CERTAIN Hunter once, said *Damna*, pursuing his Discourse, espied, in the Middle of a Field, a Fox, who looked with so engaging an Aspect, and had on a Skin so fair and lovely, that he had a great Desire to take him alive. With this Intent he found out his Hole, and, just before the Entrance into it, dug a very deep Trench, which he covered with slender Twigs and Straw and, having laid on it a Piece of smoaking Lamb's Flesh, just cut up, went and hid himself in a Corner out of sight. The Fox returning to his Hole, and observing, at a Distance, what the Hunter had left for his Breakfast, presently ran to see what dainty Morsel it was. When he came to the Trench, he would fain have been tasting the delicate Entertainment; but the Fear of some Treachery would not permit him to fall to: And, in short, finding he had strong Reasons to suspect some ill Design towards him, he was cunning enough to remove his Lodging, and take up other Quarters. In a Moment after her was gone, as Fortune would have it, came a hungary Leopard, who, being tempted by the savoury Odour of the yet warm and smoaking Flesh, made such haste to fall to, that he tumbled into the Trench. The Hunter, hearing the Noise of the falling Leopard, immediately threw himself into the Trench, without looking into it, never questioning but that it was the Fox he had taken; but there found, instead of him, the Leopard, who tore him in Pieces, and devoured him.

This Fable teaches us, that, however earnstly we may wish for any Event, Providence and Wisdom ought to regulate our Desires. I did very ill indeed, replied *Cohotorbe*, to accept the Lion's Offer of Favour and Friendship, and now heartily wish I had been content with a humbler Fortune. 'Tis not enough, replied *Damna*, interrupting him, to repent and bewail your past Life; your business is now to endeavour to moderate the Lion's Passion. I am assured of his natural Good-will to me, replied *Cohotorbe*; but Traitors and Flatterers will do their utmost to change his Favour into Hatred, and I am afraid they will bring about their Designs. Don't you remember that the Wolf, the Fox and the Raven, once ruined the Camel.

F A B L E XX.

The WOLF, *the* FOX, *the* RAVEN *and the* CAMEL.

IN former Ages, continued *Cohotorbe*, there were a crafty Raven, a subtle Fox, and a bloody Wolf, who put themselves into the Service of a Lion, that held his Court in a Wood, near a certain not-much-frequented Highway. Near this Place, a Merchant's Camel once, quite tired with long Travel, got rid of his Burden, and lay down to rest himself, and, if possible, preserve his Life. In a few Days after, having recovered his Strength, he rose up, and, ignorant of the Governor of these Territories, entered into the Lion's Wood, with a Design to feed. But, before he had spent an Hour travelling into it, he was astonished with the Appearance of the Lion, whose majestic Gait and Aspect soon informed our Traveller that he was Monarch of the Place. The Camel, who, at first Sight, expected nothing but to be devoured, was rejoiced to find this, and humbly offered him his Service. The Lion accepted it; and, after he knew by what Accident he came into the Place, asked him what he would chuse to do? Whatever your Majesty pleases, replied the Camel, very submissively. Thou art at thy Liberty, replied the Lion, to return, if thou likest it, and be the Slave of thy former Master; or if thou wilt rather live with me, thou hast my sacred and inviolable Promise that thou shalt be secure from all Injuries. The Camel was very glad of this, and remained with the Lion, doing nothing but feed without Disturbance, so that he soon became plump and fat.

One Day, after this, the Lion, in his hunting, met an Elephant, with whom he encountered; and returning wounded to the Wood, at length he was starved to Death. While he lay on his Death-bed, however the Raven, the Wolf, and the Fox, who lived only upon what the Lion left after he had been at the Field, fell into a deep Melancholy; which the Lion perceiving, said to them, I am more sorry for your Sadness than for my own Wounds. Go, and see if you can meet with any Venison in the Purloins adjoining; if you do, return and give me Notice, and, notwithstanding my Wounds, I will go and seize it for you. Upon this, away they went, left the Lion, and held a Council all three together. Said the Wolf, If I may speak among you, Friends, what Good does this Camel do here? We have no Correspondence with him; nor does the Lion get any thing by him; let us kill him, and he will keep us alive for two or three Days, and, by that time, the King may perhaps be cured of his Wounds. This Advice, however, tho'Hunger much pleaded in its Favour, did not please the Fox, who affirmed that the Camel's Life could not be justly taken away, since the Lion had given his Word and solemn Promise that he should live unmolested in the Wood; for that such an Action would render the King odious to all Posterity, who would look upon him as a perfidious Monarch, who gave Protection to a Stranger in his Dominions, only to put him to death without a Cause, whenever he could make an Advantage of his Destruction.

On this, the Raven, who had as hungry a Belly as the Wolf, together with a great deal of Wit, and as much Malice, took upon him to reconcile both these Opinions, saying, That there might be a fair Pretence found to colour the Death of the Camel. Stay here, continued he, till I return, and I will bring you the Lion's Consent of his Destruction. So saying, away he went to the Lion; and, when he came into his Pesence, making a profound Reverence, and putting on a starved and meager Look, said, May it please your Majesty to hear me a few Words: We are almost famished to Death, and so weak that we can hardly crawl along; but we have found out a Remedy for all this, and, if your Majesty will but give leave, have contrived how we shall have a Feast. What is your Remedy? answered the Lion, hardly able to open his Jaws for Weakness and Anguish; and what the Feast you propose yourselves? To whom the Raven replied, Sir, the Camel, whom you once met with in the Wood, lives like a Hermit in your Kingdom; he never comes near us, nor is he good for any thing but to satisfy our Hunger. And in regard your Majesty wants good and wholesome Diet in your present weak Condition, I am Surgeon enough to venture to assure you, that Camel's Flesh must be very proper for you. The Lion, who was of a truly noble Disposition, was highly incensed at this Proposal of the Raven, and very passionately exclaimed, Oh! what a wicked and treacherous Age is this! Vile and cunning as you are, for I have long known you, *Corvo* (for so was the Raven called) how can all your Sophistry prove it lawful in a King to be faithless, and violate ascertained Promises? Sir, replied the Raven, far be it from me to attempt to prove that; but, may it please your Majesty, I cannot but remember, upon this most urgent Occasion, that great Casuists hold it for a Maxim, that a single Person may be sacrificed to the Welfare of a whole Nation. Or, should not this be entirely satisfactory to your Majesty, perhaps there may be some Expedient found to disengage you from your Promise. Upon that, the Lion bowed down his Head with Fatigue and Anguish, as if to consider of it, and the Raven returned to his Companions, to whom he related what Discourse had passed between the King and him. And now, said he, let us go to the Camel, and inform him of the unfortunate Accident that has befallen the King, and of his being likely to starve; and then lay before him, that since we have spent the greatest Part of our Lives in Peace and Plenty under the King's Reign, it is but just that some of us now should surrender up our own, to prolong his Days.

In pursuance of this Discourse, we will engage the Camel to accompany us, and go to the King and offer him our three Carcases; striving at the same time, which shall be most free of his Flesh to serve his Majesty for his present Nourishment. The Camel, perhaps, will then be willing to follow our Example, and offer to sacrifice himself in the same manner, and then we'll take him at his Word. This they all readily agreed to; and , in short acted their Parts so well, that they took the Camel with them to the King, to whom the Raven thus addressed himself: Sir, said he, seeing your Health is of much more Consequence to the public Good, and more precious to us than our own Lives, suffer me to shew the just Sense I have of my Duty, by offering up my own Body to you, to appease your raging Hunger. What a goodly Collation you offer to his Majesty! cry'd the Fox, well instructed in the Part he was to act in this Design; you that have only a little Skin, and three or four dry Bones, are a precious Bit to satisfy the King, who, I warrant you, could feed at this time like a Glutton after a three Days Fast. I have better Flesh, and more substantial than yours, and have so much true Sense of my Duty (as I hope every one of his Majesty's Subjects has, especially those who, like us, have tasted of his Favours) that I am as desirous as yourself to approve my Gratitude and Love to my Sovereign. And turning to the Lion, Sir, said he, let me intreat your Majesty to eat me. After these, the Wolf play's his Part. Sir, said he, your Majesty must have more solid Diet to refresh your hungry Stomach than these can afford you, and I think myself a Banquet much more proper to regale you. The Camel, on this, unwilling to appear less affectionate than the rest, when it came to his turn, All you three, said he, are not enough to satisfy the King's Hunger; but, though he had not eaten a Mouthful these three Days, I alone am sufficient to restore him to his Health. Then said all the rest, this Camel speaks Reason, his Flesh is excellent, dainty, and worth your Majesty's Taste. How happy will he be to leave to Posterity such an Example of Zeal and Generosity! And, so saying, they all fell upon him, and tore him to Pieces before he could speak another Word.

This Fable shews you, that when several Conspirators combine together in the Contrivance of an Enterprize, they easily bring it to pass. You are perfectly in the Right, said *Damna*; and, for my part, were I in your Condition, I would defend my Life; and, if I must perish fall like a Warrior, not like a Victim of Justice at the Gallows. He that dies with his Sword in his Hand, renders himself famous. 'Tis not good to begin a War; but, when we are attacked, 'ti ignominious, to surrender ourselves cowardly into the Enemy's Hand. This is right and proper Counsel, replied *Cohotorbe*; but we ought to know our Strength before we engage in a Combat; For, if we attack our Enemy rashly and imprudently, we may, too late, perhaps, remember the famous Story of the Angel Ruler of the Sea, which I'll tell you.

F A B L E XXI.

The ANGEL RULER *of the* SEA, *and two Birds, called* GERANDI*.

Two Birds, of that kind called Gerandi, continued *Cohotorbe*, once lived together upon the Shores of the *Indian* Sea. After they had long enjoyed the Pleasures of conjugal Affection, when it was near the Season for laying Eggs, said the Female to the Male, 'tis time for me to chuse a proper Place wherein to produce my young ones. To whom the Male replied, This where we now are is, I think, a very good Place. No, replied the Female, this cannot do; for the Sea may hereafter swell beyond these Bounds, and the Waves carry away my Eggs. That can never be, said the Male, nor dares the Angel Ruler of the Sea do me an Injury; for, if he should, he knows I would certainly call him to an Account. You must never boast, replied the Female, of a thing which you are not able to perform. What Comparison is there between you and the Prince of the Sea? Take my Advice: Avoid such Quarrels; and, if you despise my Admonitions, beware you are not ruined by your Obstinancy. Remember the Misfortune that befel the Tortoise. 'Tis a Story I have not heard, replied the Male; pray tell it to me.

---

* Gerandi are Birds of the *East Indies*, which lay their Eggs in the Sands on the Sea-shore, and sit four Weeks.

F A B L E XXII.

The TORTOISE and two DUCKS.

THERE was a Tortoise, continued the Female, that lived in a
Pond with some Ducks, her old Companions, in full Content
and great Felicity for many Years. But, at length, there
happened so dry a Season, that there was, at last, no Water
in the Pond. The Ducks, upon this, finding themselves
constrained to remove to some other Habitation, went to the
Tortoise to take their Leaves of him. The Tortoise, in
Terror for his impending Destruction, upbraided them for
leaving him in the Time of his Calamity, and besought them
to carry him along with them. To whom the ducks replied,
Be assured 'tis a great Trouble to us that we must leave you
in this Condition, but we are constrained to it for our own
Preservation: And as to what you propose to us, to take you
with us, we have a long Journey to make, and you can never
follow us, because you cannot fly. On this Condition,
however, it is possible for us to save you, if you can only be
enough your own Friend to follow our Advice, and keep a
strict and perfect Silence, and on this Condition, if you will
promise us not to speak a Word by the Way, we will carry
you. But we shall meet with some that will talk to us, and
then, 'tis Ten to One, but you will be twatling; and if you
are, remember that we now tell you, beforehand, it will be
your Destruction. No; answered the Tortoise, fear me not; I
will do whatever you will have me. Things being thus
settled, the Ducks ordered the Tortoise to take a little Stick
and hold it by the Middle fast in his Mouth; and then,
exhorting him to keep steady, they took the Stick by each
End, and so raised him up. Thus they carried him along in
Triumph; but it was not long before, as they flew over a
Village, the Inhabitants, wondering at the Novelty of the
Sight, fell a shouting with all their Might; this made such a
Noise that the Tortoise grew impatient to be twatling; and,
at length, not able to keep Silence any longer, he was going
to wish the People's Mouths sewed up, for making such a
Clamour; but, so soon as he opened his Mouth to vent his
Curses, he let go the Stick, and so fell to the Ground and
killed himself.

This Example shews us, Spouse, said the female Gerandi,

that we ought not to despise the Exhortations of Friends. I
have heard your Fable, said the Male, and all that I shall say
in answer to it is this, *They who want Courage are no way capable
of great Performances*. Be governed by me; I have as earnest a
Desire of preserving our young ones as yourself, yet I am
bold to say, let us hatch our young ones in this Place; and be
assured, that the Angel Ruler of the Sea dares do us no
Harm. The Female, on this, obey'd, and built her Nest
accordingly in the Sand by the Seaside. But, within a Day or
two after, the Ocean swelling, the Waves overturned the
Nest, and the Ruler of the Sea took the Eggs. The Female,
on this Misfortune, addressing herself to the Male, said, I
told you that you were too vain-glorious to dare to out-brave
a Power which it becomes you rather to revere; but, now he
has done this Injury, let us see how you will revenge
yourself. Depend upon it, replied the Male, I will make him
restore your Eggs; and so saying, without Delay, he flew to
all the Birds, one after another, told them the Story and
crav'd their Aid to revenge himself upon the Ruler of the
Sea. All the Birds promised their Succour to the Gerandi,
and went with him to the Griffin, and threatened to
acknowledge him no longer for their King, if he did not
hear them in this Enterprize. The Griffin, as tenacious of
the Right of his Subjects, as revengeful in his own Nature,
readily engaged in the War, and immediately flew before
them, and they beset the Ruler of the Sea's Palace; who,
seeing such an infinite Number of Birds, in great Terror
and Affright, came out to them, and restored the Eggs.

An Enemy, said *Damna*, I very well know, is at no time to
be despised. However, replied *Cohotorbe*, I will not begin the
Combat; but, if the Lion attack me, I will endeavour to
defend myself. Well, answered *Damna*, that you may know
when to be upon your Guard, let me give you this Caution;
when you see him lash the Ground with his Tail, and roll his
Eyes angrily about, you may be sure he will immediately be
upon you. I thank you for your Advice, replied *Cohotorbe*,
and when I observe the Signs which you have, so like a
Friend, informed me of, I shall prepare myself to receive
him.

Here they parted; and *Damna*, overjoyed at the Success of
his Enterprize, ran to *Kalila*, who asked him how his Design
went forward. I thank my Fates, cried *Damna*, I am just
going to triumph over my Enemy. After this short

Confabulation, the two Foxes went to Court, where soon after *Cohotorbe* arrived.

The Lion no sooner beheld him, but he thought him guilty: And *Cohotorbe*, casting his Eyes upon the Lion, made no question, from what he saw, but that his Majesty had resolved his Ruin: So that both the one and the other manifesting those Signs which *Damna* had described to each, there began, a most terrible Combat, wherein the Lion killed the Ox, but not, however, without a great deal of Trouble and Hazard. When all was over, O! what a wicked Creature thou art! cried *Kalila* to *Damna*, thou hast here, for thine own Sake, endangered the King's Life: Thy End will be miserable for contriving such pernicious Designs; and that which happened to a Cheat, who was the Cully of his own Knaveries, will, one Day befal thee.

F A B L E XXIII.

Two young MERCHANTS, *the one crafty, and the other without Deceit.*

Two young Merchants once left their Country, to travel together upon the account of Trade: The one was called *Sharpwit*, the other *Simpleton*. These two, in one of their first Journies, by Accident found a Bag full of Money; on which said *Sharpwit* to his Companion, Travelling, I believe, in truth, is very profitable, but it is also very painful; therefore, Brother, let us be contented with this Money which Fortune has thrown in our Way, without fatiguing ourselves any more: *Simpleton* consenting to this, they left off their Designs of travelling, and returned both to their Lodging. Before they parted, *Simpleton* bethought himself of dividing what they had found, to the end they might be both at their own Liberty. But, said *Sharpwit*, No, Brother, believe me, it is much better to put it into a safe Place, and every Day to take something out of the Stock for our Occasions, without bringing the whole of our several Fortunes into separate Danger. To this *Simpleton* answered, That he very well approved of his Proposal; and, accordingly, they hid the Money, taking each of them only a small Sum for their particular Expences. The next Day, however, *Sharpwit* went where the Money lay, and having taken it away, returned home. On the other hand, *Simpleton* thought not of going to the Hoard while his little Stock lasted; but when he had expended all that he had, he went to *Sharpwit's* Lodging, and meeting with him, Come, said he, let us go together, and take out such another Sum as we took out before. Content, answered *Sharpwit*, for I have spent all my Stock, and want Money. So they went both together; but when they came to the Place where the Money had been hid, behold the Birds were flown. *Sharpwit* on this threw himself on the Ground, tore his Hair, rent his Cloaths, and weeping to his Companion, Why hast thou dealt so unkindly with thy Friend, said he, for nobody but you could take away the Money, since nobody else knew where it was hid. 'Twas in vain for *Simpleton* to swear he had not taken it away: The other still feigned to be assured of the contrary, and wickedly, not contented with robbing his Brother of all he had, was for having him lose his Life by false Accusations, that he might be sure to have no more Fear of his finding him out. What will not the wicked Thirst after Money compel us to! To conclude, at length, they went both before a Judge, before whom *Sharpwit*, after he had related the whole Story, how they found the Money, and how they agreed to hide it, accused *Simpleton* of having stolen it. The Judge called presently for Witnesses to prove the Robbery; to which *Sharpwit* replied, I have no other Witnesses but the Tree that grows next the Place; and I hope God, who is just, will suffer the dumb Tree to give Testimony of the Truth. The Judge, admiring to hear the Man talk at such a rate, reselved to see the Issue of the Business, and accepting the Tree for a Witness, promised the next Day to take a Walk to the Tree and examine it: And so the two Merchants went home. In the mean time *Sharpwit* told his Father the whole Story, assuring him withal, that he had no Hope but in him, when he took the Tree for his Evidence. And if you will but act your Part, added he, we shall have the Sum which I have taken to ourselves, and as much more from the Party accused upon his Condemnation, which will serve us very well the Remainder of our Days. His Father, on this, asked him what he was to do: Why, Sir, reply'd the Son, you must go into the Tree in the Evening, and lie there all Night, to the end that when the Judge comes betimes in the Morning, you may give Testimony according to the Custom. O Son! said the Father, leave off these Schemes of Knavery, for though thou may'st deceive Men, thou can'st never deceive the Almighty; and I am afraid thy Fortune will have the same Success with that of the Frog.

F A B L E XXIV.

The FROG, *the* CRAY-FISH, *and the* SERPENT.

THERE was once a Frog which had her Habitation in the Neighbourhood of the Hole of a Serpent, who every time she brought forth young ones, eat them up; this put her almost beside her Wits; and one Day going to pay a Visit to a Cray-fish, that was one of her Gossips, in the Anguish of her Heart she utter'd many bitter Imprecations against the Serpent, and made her the Confidant of her Grievances. The Cray-fish put her in good heart, assuring her, that a way might be found out to rid her from such a pernicious Neighbour. You will oblige me indeed, said the Frog, if you will teach me that. Hark you then, replied the Cray-fish, there is in such a Place one of my Comrades, who is very large, and indeed a Monster among us; take you a sufficient Number of little Menows, and lay them all in a Row from the Cray-fish's Hole, to the Serpent's Lodging; for the Cray-fish that I tell you of will certainly snap them up all, one after another, till he comes where the Serpent lies, who will come forth upon the Noise, and then the Cray-fish will devour him too. The Frog followed this Advice, and tasted the sweet Pleasure of Revenge. But two Days after, the

Cray-fish that had eaten the Serpent, thinking to find more, went hunting in the same Neighbourhood, and soon fell upon the Place where the Frog was now hatching another Brood, and eat up not only all her young ones, but herself also.

You see by this Fable, concluded he, that Deceivers are often deceived. Father, said the Son, let me interest you to leave off this idle Discourse; we have no time now for talking, but must conclude either to earn the Money, or go without it. Upon this the old Man, who was covetous enough, not able to dissuade his Son, submitted, and went and hid himself in the Tree. The next Day, betimes in the Morning, the Judge made haste to the Tree, accompany'd by a great Number of Persons of Wit and Penetration, and a great Croud of others that desired to be Witnesses of this new way of Accusation. After some Ceremonies, the Judge ask'd the Tree, Whether it were true that *Simpleton* had taken the Money in dispute? Presently he heard a Voice that answer'd, *Yes, — he is guilty of what he is accus'd.* This somewhat astonish'd the Judge at first; but afterwards surmising that there might be somebody in the Tree, ordered all the Boughs round about the Tree to be heap'd together and set on fire. Upon which the poor old Man, after he had endured the Heat as long as he could, cry'd out, Mercy, Mercy; and being then lifted out of the Tree, confessed the Truth, made manifest the Innocence of *Simpleton* and *Sharpwit's* Wickedness; for which he was punish'd as he deserv'd, while all the Money was taken from the Accuser and given to the Party accused.

I have recited this Example to you, said *Kalila*, to shew you, that there is nothing like acting with Uprightness and Sincerity. You are to blame, said *Damna*, to call Wit by the Name of Knavery, and the Care of a Man's own Interests by the Appellation of Artifice: For my part, I am apt to think, that I have shewed nothing but Wit and Judgment in my whole Conduct. Thou art a wicked Creature, cried *Kalila*, nor will I any longer listen to thee, or live with thee; thou teachest such wicked Maxims, that those who frequent thy Company, I am afraid, will come to the same End with a certain Gardener, of whom I'll tell thee a remarkable History.

F A B L E XXV.

The GARDENER and the BEAR.

THERE was once, in the Eastern Parts of our Country, a Gardener, who loved Gardening to that degree, that he wholly absented himself from the Company of Men, to the end he might give himself up entirely to the Care of his Flowers and Plants. He had neither Wife nor Children; and from Morning till Night he did nothing but work in his Garden, so that it lay like a terrestrial Paradise. At length, however, the good Man grew weary of being alone, and took a Resolution to leave his Garden in search of good Company.

As he was, soon after, walking at the Foot of a Mountain, he spy'd a Bear, whose Looks had in them nothing of the savage Fierceness natural to that Animal, but were mild and gentle. This Bear was also weary of being alone, and came down from the Mountain, for no other Reason, but to see whether he could meet with any one that would join Society with him. So soon therefore as these two saw each other, they began to have a Friendship one for another; and the Gardener first accosted the Bear, who, in return, made him a profound Reverence. After some Compliments pass'd between them, the Gardener made the Bear a Sign to follow him; and carrying him into his Garden, regal'd him with a World of very delicious Fruit, which he had carefully preserved; so that at length they enter'd into a very strict Friendship together; insomuch, that when the Gardener was weary of working, and lay down to take a little Nap, the Bear, out of Affection, stay'd all the while by him, and kept off the Flies from his Face. One Day as the Gardener lay down to sleep at the Foot of a Tree, and the Bear stood by, according to his Custom, to drive away the Flies, it happened that one of those Insects did light upon the Gardener's Mouth, and still as the Bear drove it away from one Side, it would light on the other; which put the Bear into such a Passion, that he took up a great Stone to kill it. 'Tis true, he did kill the Fly, but at the same time he broke out two or three of the Gardener's Teeth. From whence Men of Judgment observe, *That it is better to have a prudent Enemy, than an ignorant Friend.*

This Example shews, that we should take care whom we are concern'd with; and I am of Opinion that your Society is no less dangerous than the Company of the Bear. This is an ill Comparison, reply'd *Damna*, I hope I am not so ignorant, but that I am able to distinguish between what is baneful, and what is beneficial to my Friend, Why, I know very well, indeed, reply'd *Kalila*, that your Transgressions are not the Failings of Ignorance; but I know too that you can betray your Friends, and that when you do, it is not without long Premeditation; witness the Contrivances you made use of to set the Lion and the poor Ox together by the Ears: But, after this, I cannot endure to hear you pretend to Innocence. In short, you are like the Man that would make his Friend believe that Rats eat Iron.

F A B L E XXVI.

The MERCHANT and his FRIEND.

A CERTAIN Merchant, said *Kalila*, pursuing her Discourse, had once a great Desire to make a long Journey. Now in regard that he was not very wealthy, 'tis requisite, said he to himself, that before my Departure I should leave some Part of my Estate in the City, to the end that if I meet with ill Luck in my Travels, I may have wherewithal to keep me at my Return. To this Purpose he delivered a great Number of Bars of Iron, which were a principal Part of his Wealth, in trust to one of his Friends, desiring him to keep them during his Absence; and then taking his Leave, away he went. Some time after, having had but ill Luck in his Travels, he returned home; and the first thing he did was to go to his Friend, and demand his Iron: But his Friend, who owed several Sums of Money, having sold the Iron to pay his own Debts, made him this Answer: Truly, Friend, said he, I put your Iron into a Room that was close lock'd, imagining it would have been there as secure as my own Gold; but an Accident has happened which nobody could have suspected, for there was a Rat in the Room that eat it all up. The Merchant, pretending Ignorance, replied, 'tis a terrible Misfortune to me indeed, but I know of old that Rats love Iron extremely; I have suffered by them many times before in the same Manner, and therefore can the better bear my present Affliction. This Answer extremely pleased the Friend, who was glad to hear the Merchant so well inclined to believe that the Rats had eaten his Iron; and to remove all Suspicions, desired him to dine with him the next Day. The Merchant promised he would, but in the mean time he met in the Middle of the City one of his Friend's Children; the Child he carried home, and locked up in a Room. The next Day he went to his Friend, who seem'd to be in great Affliction, which he ask'd him the Cause of, as if he had been perfectly ignorant of what had happened. Oh my dear Friend! answered the other, I beg you to excuse me, if you do not see me so cheerful as otherwise I would be; I have lost one of my Children; I have had him cried by Sound of Trumpet, but I know not what is become of him. Oh! replied the Merchant, I am grieved to hear this, for Yesterday in the Evening, as I parted from hence, I saw and Owl in the Air, with a Child in his Claws, but whether it were yours I cannot tell. Why you most foolish and absurd Creature, replied the Friend, are you not ashamed to tell such an egregious Lye? An Owl, that weighs, at most, not above two or three Pounds, can he carry a Boy that weighs above fifty? Why, replied the Merchant, do you make such a Wonder at that? as if in a Country where one Rat can eat an hundred Ton Weight of Iron, it were such a Wonder for an Owl to carry a Child that weighs not above fifty Pounds in all. The Friend, upon this, found that the Merchant was no such Fool as he took him to be, begged his Pardon for the Cheat which he designed to have put upon him, restored him the Value of his Iron, and so had his Son again.

This Fable shews, continued *Kalila*, that these fine-spun Deceits are not always successful; but as to your Principles, I can easily see that if you could be so unjust as to deceive the Lion, to whom you were so much indebted for a thousand Kindnesses, you will with much more Confidence put your Tricks upon those to whom you are less obliged. This is the Reason why I think your Company is dangerous.

While *Damna* and *Kalila* were thus confabulating together, the Lion, whose Passion was now over, made great Lamentations for *Cohotorbe*, saying, that he began to be sensible of his Loss, because of his extraordinary Endowments. I know not, added he, whether I did ill or well in destroying him, or whether what was reported of him was true or false. Thus musing for a while in a studious Melancholy, at length he repented of having punished a Subject, who might, for aught he knew, be innocent. *Damna*, observing that the Lion was seized with Remorse of Conscience, left *Kalila*, and accosted the King with a most respectful Humility: Sir, said he, what makes your Majesty so pensive? Consider, that here your Enemy lies at your Feet, and fix your Eyes upon such an Object with Delight. When I think upon *Cohotorbe's* Virtues, said the Lion, I cannot but bemoan his Loss. He was my Support and my Comfort, and it was by his prudent Counsel that my People lived in Repose. This indeed was once the Case, replied *Damna*, but his Revolt was therefore the more dangerous; and I am grieved to see your Majesty bewail the Death of an unfaithful Subject. 'Tis true he was profitable to the Public; but in regard he had a Design upon your Person, you have done no more than what the wisest have already advised, which is to cut off a Member that would prove the Destruction of the whole Body. These Admonitions of *Damna's* for the present gave the Lion a little Comfort: But notwithstanding all, *Cohotorbe's* Innocence crying continually afterwards in the Monarch's Breast for Vengeance, rouzed at last some Thoughts in him, by which he found means to discover the long Chain of Villanies *Damna* had been guilty of. *He that will reap Wheat must never sow Barley. He only that does good Actions, and thinks just Thoughts, will be happy in this World, and cannot fail of Rewards and Blessings in the other.*

C H A P. III.

That the W I C K E D *come to an ill End.*

I HAVE with great Attention and Delight, said *Dabschelim*, now heard the History of a Sycophant, who by his Flatteries deceived his Prince, and was the Cause that he wronged his Minister: Tell me therefore now how the Lion came to discover *Damna's* Infidelities, and what was the End of this cunning and most wicked Fox.

Kings, answered the old *Bramin*, are by no means to give any Credit to the various Reports that are whispered in their Ears, till they understand whether the Stories which they hear proceed from the Lips of Friends or Enemies. It is with great Delight that I have observed your Majesty's Attention to what I have been relating, and now shall joyfully proceed to give the Account of those Things which you yet desire to know. Some time after the Lion had killed the Ox, he was, as I have already observed, very much troubled in his Mind; the Reflections that he continually made upon the good Services which the Ox had done him, plunged him into so deep a Melancholy, that he abandoned the Care of his Dominions, and his Court became a Wilderness. He talked, without Intermission, of *Cohotorbe's* rare Endowments; and the good Character which others gave him was the only Consolation which his Grief would admit. One Night as he was wrapt up in Discourse with the Leopard concerning the Virtues of the Ox; Your Majesty, said the Leopard, too heavily afflicts yourself for a Thing which it is impossible to remedy: And suffer me to remind your Majesty, that he that turmoils himself to seek what he cannot find, not only never acquires what he seeks, but instead of that loses what he has; as the Fox once lost a Hide, in hopes of getting a Hen which he longed for: 'Tis a remarkable Story, and if your Majesty will give me Permission, I will relate it to you.

F A B L E I.

The FOX, *the* WOLF, *and the* RAVEN.

A CERTAIN Fox that was ranging about in search of Food, found once a large Piece of a raw Hide, which some wild Beast or other had let fall; he eat one Part of it, and took the rest with a Design to carry it to his Hole; but in his Way near a Village he spied several Hens that were plump and fat, which a certain Boy set to watch them had always in his Eye. These Dainties set the Fox's Teeth a watering to that Degree, that he left his raw Hide, which he was sure of, to get one of these delicate Morsels. At the same Instant came a Wolf up to him, and asked him what he gazed after with so much Earnestness. Those Hens that you see yonder, answered the Fox; I would fain have one of them for my second Course. You will only lose your Time, replied the Wolf, in attemping it; they are guarded by so vigilant a Servant, that 'tis impossible for you to get near them, without running a manifest Hazard. Take my Advice therefore, content yourself with your Piece of raw Hide, for fear you meet with the same hard Fortune that once befel the Ass, who, while he was looking after his Tail, lost his Ears.

FABLE II.

The ASS *and the* GARDENER.

A CERTAIN Ass, continued he, had once by some Accident lost his Tail, which was a grievous Affliction to him; and as he was every where seeking after it, being Fool enough to think he could set it on again, he passed through a Meadow and afterwards got into a Garden. The Gardener seeing him, and not able to endure the Mischief he was doing in trampling down his Garden, fell into a violent Rage, ran to the Ass, and never standing on the Ceremony of a Pillory, cut off both his Ears, and beat him out of the Ground. Thus the Ass, who bemoaned the Loss of his Tail, was in far greater Affliction when he saw himself without Ears: And believe me, that, in general, whoever he be that takes not Reason for his Guide, wanders about, and at length falls into Precipices.

The Fox however was still eagerly importuned by his extraordinary longing after a Tit-bit. What come you hither for, said he to the Wolf, to trouble me with your Morals and your Fables? I will let you see, that he who has Courage scorns the Terror of such Examples, and dares do any thing: So saying, he advanced slily towards the Hens, leaving his Piece of raw Hide; and the Wolf finding that his Admonitions would do no Good, went about his Business. In the mean time the Fox crept softly toward his feather'd Prey; but the Boy perceiving his thievish Intention, threw a large Stone so luckily at him, that he hit him on the Foot. The poor Fox afraid lest the Boy should reach his Pate next time, returned with much more Haste than he came, resolved to be contented with his Piece of raw Hide. But, alas! that was gone too; for a Raven coming by at the same time, had carried it away; and the Fox could now have torn his own Flesh for Madness.

You see, Sir, pursued the Leopard, by these Stories the Misfortunes that attend rash and inconsiderate Enterprizes; and permit me to add, that your Majesty ought never to despair, nor abandon the Government of your Dominions for the Loss of one Subject. On this the Lion for a while stood mute, but then recovering his Speech, You say true, said he, but if I do not this, I would at least ease my troubled Mind, and strongly revenge *Cohotorbe's* Death, if I could find that he had been unjustly accused. This is a just and a noble Intent, replied the Leopard; but, Sir, desponding is not the way to attain your End: You must carefully examine whether the Complaints that were brought you of his Miscarriages were true or not. If he was guilty, he has been deservedly punished; if not, the Accuser ought to feel your Severity. Then said the Lion to the Leopard, I appoint thee my Searcher of the Truth on this Occasion, and entreat thee to do all thou can'st to find it out.

Now in regard it was by this time late, the Leopard for the present took his Leave of the Lion: But in his way to his Lodging, passing by *Kalila* and *Damna's* Apartment, he thought he heard them discoursing together. The Leopard had long suspected *Damna* to be no less wicked than indeed he was, and his Curiosity therefore led him to go near and listen. *Kalila,* as Fortune would have it, was at this very time upbraiding her Husband with his Perfidiousness, his Dissimulation, and all the Atirfices he had made use of to ruin *Cohotorbe.* The Leopard, fully informed by her Reproaches of *Damna's* Treasons, went immediately away to the Lion's Mother, to whom he related what he had heard; and she presently hasting to her Son, cried to him, You have Reason indeed to be afflicted for the Loss of *Cohotorbe* your Favourite, for he died innocent. What Proof have you of this? demanded the Lion eagerly. Pardon me, answered the Mother, if I am not so hasty to reveal a Secret which may, if too suddenly related to you, inflame your Anger to too high a Degree, and prejudice the Person that has intrusted me. But I beseech you listen to this Fable.

F A B L E III.

The PRINCE *and his* MINISTER.

THERE was once a Prince who was very much famed throughout all these Countries; he was a great Conqueror, and was potent, rich, and just. One Day as he rode a hunting, said he to his Minister, Put on thy best speed, I will run my Horse against thine, that we may see which is the swiftest: I have a long time had a strange Desire to make this Trial. The Minister, in obedience to his Master, put on his Horse, and rode full speed, and the King followed him. But when they were got at a great Distance from the Grandees and Nobles that accompanied them, the King, stopping his Horse, said to his Minister, I had no other Design in this, but to bring thee to a Place where we might be alone; for I have a Secret to impart to thee, having found thee more faithful than any other of my Servants. I have a Jealousy that the Prince my Brother is framing some Contrivance against my Person, and for that Reason, I have made choice of thee to prevent him; but be discreet. The Minister on this swore he would be true to him; and when they had thus agreed, they staid till the Company overtook them, who were in great Trouble for the King's Person. The Minister, however, notwithstanding his Promises to the King, upon the first Opportunity he had to speak with the King's Brother, disclosed to him the Design that was brewing to take away his Life. And this obliged the young Prince to thank him for his Information, promise him great Rewards, and take some Precautions in regard to his own Safety.

Some few Days after the King died, and his Brother succeeded him: But when the Minister who had done him his signal Service, expected now some great Preferment, the first thing he did after he was advanced to the Throne, was to order him to be put to death. The poor Wretch immediately upbraided him with the Service he had done him. Is this, said he, the Recompence for my Friendship to you? this the Reward which you promised me? Yes, answered the new King, whoever reveals the Secrets of his Prince, deserves no less than Death; and since thou hast committed so foul a Crime, thou deservest to die. Thou betrayedst a King who put his Confidence in thee, and who loved thee above all his Court, how is it possible therefore for me to trust thee in my Service? 'Twas in vain for the Minister to alledge any Reasons in his own Justification, they would not be heard, nor could he escape the Stroke of the Executioner.

You see by this Fable, Son, continued the old Lioness, that Secrets are not to be disclosed. But, my dear Mother, answered the King, he that entrusted you with this Secret desires it should be made known, seeing he is the first that makes the Discovery: For, if he could not keep it himself, how could he desire another to be more reserved? Let me conjure you, continued he, if what you have to say be true, put me out of my Pain. The Mother seeing herself so hardly prest, then, said she, I must inform you of a Criminal unworthy of Pardon; for tho' it be the Saying of wise Men, that a King ought to be merciful, yet there are certain Crimes that never ought to be forgiven. 'Tis *Damna* I mean, pursued the Matron Lioness, who, by his false Insinuations, wrought *Cohotorbe's* Fall. And having so said, she retired, leaving the Lion in a deep Astonishment; some time he pondered with himself on this Discovery, and afterwards summoned an Assembly of the whole Court. *Damna* taking Umbrage at this (as guilty Consciences always make People Cowards) comes to one of the King's Favourites, and asks him if he knew the Reason of the

Lion's calling such an Assembly? (which the Lion's Mother overhearing) Yes, said she, it is to pronounce thy Death; for thy Artifice and juggling Politics are now, tho' too late, discovered. Madam, answered *Damna*, they who render themselves worthy of Esteem and Honour at Court by their Virtues, never fail of Enemies. O! that we, added he, would act no otherwise than as the Almighty acts in regard to us; for he gives to every one according to his Desert; but we, on the other Side, frequently punish those who are worthy of Reward, and as often cherish those who deserve our Indignation. How much was I to blame to quit my Solitude, merely to consecrate my Life to the King's Service, to meet with this Reward. Whoever, continued he, dissatisfied with what he has, prefers the Service of Princes, before his Duty to his Creator, will be sure, I find, early or late to repent in vain. This your Ladyship may see by the following Story.

FABLE IV.

A Hermit *who quitted the Desert to live at Court.*

THERE was once in a remote Part of his Majesty's (my hitherto most gracious Master) Dominions, a certain Hermit, who had renounced the Pleasures of the World, and led a very austere Life in a Wilderness. His Virtue, in a small time, made such a Noise in the World, that an infinite Number of People flocked every Day to visit him, some out of Curiosity, and others to consult him upon several different Matters. The Fame of this Hermit's Wisdom and Virtue spread every Day more and more. The King of the Country, who was very devout, and who loved all virtuous and worthy Men, no sooner understood that there was in his Kingdom a Person of so much Knowledge and Goodness, but he rode to see him, made him a noble Present, and desired that he might hear some of his learned and virtuous Exhortations. On this Desire of the Monarch, the Hermit began and laid before him a most glorious Scene of true Knowledge. Sir, said he, the Almighty Governor of the Universe has two Habitations, the one perishable, which is the World, the other eternal, which is the Abode of the Blessed hereafter. 'Tis not for your Majesty, therefore, to dote upon the Felicities of the Earth; you ought to aspire to those eternal Treasures, the meanest Part of which is of a nobler Value than all the Principalities of the World: Try then, sacred Sir, with Earnestness to attain the Possession of those eternal Blessings, and you shall not lose the Reward of your Endeavours. The Monarch, on this, demanded by what Assiduities they might be acquired: By a Series of virtuous Actions alone, replied the Hermit, particularly by relieving the Poor, and succouring the Distressed; for of this be ever mindful, All Princes that desire to enjoy eternal Repose, must labour to give temporal Tranquility to their Subjects.

The King was so taken with this Discourse, that he took up a Resolution to spend some Hours with this good Hermit every Day, and so for the present returned to his Palace. Long continued he every Day his Visits to this Oracle of Truth: Among the rest, one Day, as the King and the Hermit were together in the Hermitage, they saw a confused Multitude of People thronging toward them, and rending the Air with the loud Cries of Justice, Justice. The Hermit went to the Door of the Cave, and bad them draw near, examined them; and, having understood their Differences, made a quick and peaceful Accommodation between them, sending them away all praying for a thousand Blessings on him. The King, upon this, admiring the Hermit's Prudence and Dispatch, desired him that he would favour him so far, as for the Sake of the public Good, sometimes to leave his tranquil Abode for a few Hours, and be present in his Councils. The Hermit readily agreed to this, believing he might be beneficial to the Poor. And after this was frequently in those Assemblies; and the King ever pronounced his Decrees according to his Judgment, insomuch, that at length he became so necessary, that nothing was done in the Kingdom without his Advice.

The Hermit now beginning to find that Men made their Addresses to him, began to forget his determined Solitude and Humility, and soon took upon him the Rank and Quality of Chief Minister. To which End, he provided himself with a rich Livery and a numerous Train. He now forgot his Austerities, his Penances, and his Prayers, and looking upon himself as one that would be greatly missed in the Government, took great care of his own Person, lay soft, and fed upon the most exquisite Dainties: And the King, who was very well satisfied with the Hermit, let him do as he pleased, and, in short, discharged upon his Shoulders the whole Burden of his Cares.

One Day another Hermit, a Friend to him that lived at Court, came to visit his Brother, with whom he had frequently spent whole Nights in Prayer, and whole Days in Fasting and Penitence, was astonished to see him arrayed in costly Habits, and environed with a great Number of Servants; reserving his Patience, however, till Night locked up all the Court in dark Retirement; when all was hushed, accosting the Courtier-Hermit in the most pathetic Manner, Oh, my dear Friend, said he, in what a Condition do I find you? What a strange Alteration is this? and what is now become of all the Sanctity that you used to pretend to? The Court-Hermit would fain have excused himself, by saying, That he was constrained to keep so great a Train: But his Brother, who was a Person of Wit and Judgment, said, these Excuses are the Dictates of Sensuality; I see that Wealth and Preferments have enchanted your Devotion. What Demon has put you out of Conceit with your praying Life? and why, forgetting the Duties of a retired Station, do you here prefer Noise before Silence, and Tumult before Ease? Think not, answered the Court-Hermit, that the Business of the Court is any Hindrance to me from continuing my Devotions; no, Brother, I continue them with more than wanted Fervour, and hourly return my humble Thanks to Heaven for placing me in a Station where I may do Good to the World. You deceive yourself, replied the Brother Hermit, to think that your Prayers can be heard, while you are environed with the Cares and Pomps of the World, as they were, when holy and heavenly Duties took up all your time; no, no, I adjure you therefore, take my Advice, break these Chains of Gold that bind you to the Court, and return to your Desert; otherwise, be assured, you will, at last, meet with the cruel Destiny of the blind Man, who despised the Council of his Friend.

F A B L E V.

The BLIND MAN *who travelled with one of his* FRIENDS.

THERE were once, continued he, two Men that travelled together, one of whom was blind. These two Companions being in the Course of their Journey, one time, surprized by Night upon the Road, entered into a Meadow, there to rest themselves till Morning; and as soon as Day appeared, they rose, got on Horse-back, and continued their Journey. Now, the blind Man, instead of his Whip, as ill Fate would have it, had picked up a Serpent that was stiff with Cold; but having it in his Hand, as it grew a little warm, he felt it somewhat softer than his Whip, which pleased him very much; he thought he had gained by the Change, and therefore never minded the Loss. In this Manner he travelled some time; but when the Sun began to appear and illuminate the World, his Companion perceived the Serpent, and with loud Cries, Friend, said he, You have taken up a Serpent instead of your Whip; throw it out of your Hand, before you feel the mortal Caresses of the venomous Animal. But the blind Man, no less blind in his Intellects than his Body, believing that his Friend had only jested with him to get away his Whip, What! said he, do you envy my good Luck?

I lost my Whip that was worth nothing, and here my kind Fortune has sent me a new one. Pray do not take me for such a Changeling but that I can distinguish a Serpent from a Whip. With that his Friend replied, Companion, I am obliged by the Laws of Friendship and Humanity to inform you of your Danger; and therefore let me again assure you of your Error, and conjure you, if you love your Life, throw away the Serpent. To which the blind Man, more exasperated than persuaded, said, Why do you take all this Pains to cheat me, and press me thus to throw away a thing which you intend, as soon as I have done so, to pick up yourself? His Companion, grieved at his Obstinacy, intreated him to be persuaded of the Truth, swore he had no such Design, and protested to him that what he held in his Hand was a real and poisonous Serpent. But neither Oaths nor Protestations would prevail, the blind Man would not alter his Resolution. The Sun, by this time, began to grow high, and his Beams having warmed the Serpent by degrees, he began to crawl up the blind Man's Arm, which he, immedialy after, bit in such a venomous Manner, that he gave him his Death's Wound.

This Example teaches us, Brother, continued the pious Hermit, that we ought to distrust our Senses, and that it is a difficult Task to master them, when we are in Possession of a thing that flatters our Fancy.

This apposite Fable, and judicious Admonition, awaked the Court-hermit from his pleasing Dream; he opened his Eyes, and surveyed the Hazards that he ran at Court; and bewailing the time which he had vainly spent in the Service of the World, he passed the Night in Sighs and Tears. His Friend constantly attended him, and rejoiced he had made him a Convert; but, alas! Day being come, the new Honours that were done him destroyed all his Repentance. At this melancholy Sight, the pious Stranger, with Tears in his Eyes, and many Prayers for his lost Brother, as he accounted him, took his Leave of the Court and retired to his Cell. On the other hand, the Courtier began to thrust himself into all manner of Business, and soon became unjust, like the People of the World. One day, in the Hurry of his Affairs, he rashly and inconsiderately condemned to Death a Person, who, according to the Laws and Customs of the Country, ought not to have suffered capital

Punishment. After the Execution of the Sentence, his Conscience teazed him with Reproaches that troubled his Repose for some time; and, at length, the Heirs of the Person whom he had unjustly condemned, with great Difficulty, obtained leave of the King to inform against the Hermit, whom they accused of Injustice and Oppression; and the Council, after mature Debate upon the Informations, ordered that the Hermit should suffer the same Punishment which he had inflicted upon the Person deceased. The Hermit made use of all his Credit and his Riches to save his Life. But all availed not, and the Decree of the Council was executed.

I must confess, said *Damna*, that, according to this Example I ought, long since, to have been punished for having quitted my Solitude to serve the King; notwithstanding that I can safely appeal to Heaven, that I am guilty of no Crime against any Person yet.

Damna here gave over speaking, and his Eloquence was admired by all the Court: Different Opinions were formed of him by the different Persons present. And as for the Lion, he held down his Head, turmoiled with so many various Thoughts that he knew not what to resolve, nor what Answer to give. While the Lion however was in this Dilemma, and all the Courtiers kept Silence, a certain Creature called *Siagousch*, who was one of the most faithful Servants the King had, stept forward, and spoke to this Effect:

O thou most wicked Wretch, all the Reproaches which thou throwest upon those that serve Kings, turn only to thy own Shame; for besides that it does no way belong to thee to enter into these Affairs, know that an Hour of Service done to the King is worth a hundred Years of Prayers. Many Persons of Merit have we seen, that have quitted their little Cells to go to Court, where serving Princes, they have eased the People, and secured them from tyrannical Oppressions? The Fable which I am going to tell you may serve for a Proof of what I say.

F A B L E VI.

A religious DOCTOR *and a* DERVISE.

THERE once lived in a certain City of *Persia* an ancient religious Doctor, who spent his Life wholly in his proper calling, the inculcating true Notions of Virtue, Piety and Religion into Persons of all Ranks. This excellent Man had an established Reputation throughout the Kingdom, of being a very learned and virtuous Man. He was called *Rouchan Zamir*, that is to say, *Clear Conscience*. A Dervise of great Fame once, pushed on by the Motives of an extraordinary Devotion, parted from *Mauralnachos*, a Province of *Tartary*, to visit this religious Doctor, and to consult him upon some difficult Questions. After much Fatigue he arrived at the Habitation of our Doctor: The Doctor, himself, however, was not within, but a Person that he kept as a constant Companion was there, who, observing that the Dervise was weary, desired him to rest himself; adding, that this was the Hour at which the Doctor usually returned from Court, whither he went every Day. Here all was at once destroyed; for when the Dervise heard that the religious Doctor, *Clear Conscience*, intermeddled with State Affairs, Oh! cry'd he, how sorry I am to have come so far and lost my Time and Labour, for I am very well assured that there is nothing to be learned from a Man that frequents Courts. With these Words, he departed from the Place with a very ill Opinion of the religious Doctor. Now it happened, that the Captain of the Watch was searching about that Day for a notorious Robber, who had made his Escape the Night before; and the King had threatened to put him to Death if he did not find him again. The Captain meeting the Dervise, seized him instead of the Offender whom he sought for, and without examining him, hurried him away immediately to Execution. 'Twas in vain for the Dervise to swear himself an honest Man, his Tale would not be heard, and already the Hangman had his Knife ready to take off his Head, when our religious Doctor, returning from Court, saw the Dervise in the Hands of the Executioner. The Doctor immediately ordered him to be untied, affirming him to be one of his Brethren, and that it was impossible he should have committed the Crime of which he was accused. The Executioner made a profound Reverence to the Doctor, fell upon his Knee, and kissed his Hand, and unbound the Dervise, who accompanied the Doctor to his Habitation. As they were going on, the Doctor entered on the Occasion of his present Manner of Life with his released Friend. Be not surprised, said he, that, I spend the greatest Part of my Time at Court; I live not after this Manner for the Sake of the Vanities of the World; these, believe me, Brother, I have no Taste for; no, 'tis for nobler Ends that I attend a Court. Injustice and Oppression too often reign there; these I spend my Labours to prevent, and devote my Life to what I abhor, that I may be able to rescue the Stranger from Destruction, make the Distressed be relieved, and to deliver from Death the Innocent, such as you are. The Dervise on this acknowledging, that he had made a most rash and wicked Judgment; told the Doctor, that from that time forward, he would never blame those that went to Court for good Purposes.

By this Example, added *Siagousch*, we see that the greatest Observers of the Law and truest Followers of Virtue are not always banished from the Court. 'Tis true, replied *Damna*, that sometimes most virtuous Men do live at Court; but 'tis not till after they have implored the Succour of Heaven, because they know full well, that unless Heaven particularly protect them, they must, of Necessity ruin themselves.

Besides, these People never come to Court till they have absolutely laid aside all private Interests, which is the most dangerous Rock that they can split upon. I confess, that with a Mind so free from Interest, a Man may embrace all Sorts of Conditions. But we, alas! that are not endowed with such a sublime Virtue, how shall we, with Safety to ourselves, exercise an Employment so dangerous, unless we have the good Fortune to serve just and penetrating Princes, who, being able to distinguish faithful from wicked Servants, reward and punish them according to the Rules of Justice?

On this, the Mother of the Lion rising from her Seat, with a Look of conscious Knowledge and Disdain, said, *Damna*, We all allow the Truth of what you have been saying; but, know you too, that the Assembly sits not here, but to upbraid thee for thy Perfidy to the best of Princes, and for destroying one of his most faithful Subjects. Madam, replied *Damna*, I well know what it is your Highness is pleased to hint at, but permit me to clear my Innocence, by answering, that his Majesty is not ignorant, no more than this Assembly, that there never was any Quarrel or Dispute between the Ox and me. On the other hand, all the World knows, that he was obliged to me alone for the Preferment and Dignities to which the King's Favour had advanced him. 'Tis true, that I informed his Majesty of an Attempt that was forming against his Person. It was my Duty to do this when I knew it, and I hope there is not one of all you present but would have done the same; and of this be assured, I accused none but the Guilty, and declared nothing but what I heard with my Ears, and saw with my own Eyes.

The Love and Reverence I bear my most gracious Sovereign, alone influenced me in what I have done: And I have this to satisfy my Conscience, that tho' I have bee so unhappy as to destroy my Friend, for which, pardon me, ye most illustrious Assembly, but I cannot now forbear to weep, yet I acted without Passion or Interest: For what Advantage could I reap by *Cohotorbe's* Death? The Favours which I have received from the King my Master, and the Duty I owe him, would they permit me to conceal from him such a Piece of Treason? And as for those that now accuse me, let me silence them for ever, by declaring this sacred Truth, They are only such as fear me, and seek my Life, to the end that I should not discover their Enterprises.

These Words *Damna* pronounced with such a Constancy and Presence of Mind, that the Lion knew not what to resolve. After much deliberation, We must refer this Cause, said he, to a select Number of Judges; for it is my Pleasure that this Affair be thoroughly and carefully examined. Most justly ordained, cried *Damna,* for they who judge with Precipitation, commonly judge amiss; most gladly I submit myself to such a Tribunal, and humbly adore your Majesty's Wisdom and Goodness for appointing it. My Innocence, I doubt not, in time, will clear itself, tho' a hasty Judgment might unknowingly have pronounced me guilty: Nothing ought to be decided in Things of Consequence, without having a perfect Knowledge of the Whole Affair, otherwise we may be deluded as the Woman was, whose Adventure, with your Majesty's Permission, I will relate to this august Assembly.

FABLE VII.

The MERCHANT'S WIFE *and the* PAINTER.

A MERCHANT of the City of *Catchemir* had once a very beautiful Wife, who loved and was beloved by a Painter who excelled in his Art. These two Lovers doated on each other to that degree, that they neglected no possible Opportunity to be in each other's Company. One Day, said the Mistress to her Gallant, I find that when you would speak to me, you are constrained to make a great many troublesome Signs, as counterfeiting your Voice, whistling, coughing, and the like; but I would have us learn some way to spare all this Pains. Cannot you think of some Invention that may serve us by way of a Signal? Yes, replied the Painter, I have often had it in my Thoughts, and I will now do it; I will paint two Masks, the Whiteness of one of which shall surpass the Brightness of a Star, and the Blackness of the other shall outvie the Locks of the Moor. When you see me come forth with one or the other of these Masks, you will know what they signify. The Painter's Prentice, who was no less in love with the Women than his Master, being in the next Room, heard this Agreement between the two Lovers, and resolved to make his own Advantage of it. Accordingly, soon after this, one Day when his Master was gone to draw some Lady's Picture in the City, he took the Mask of Assignation, and walked before the House of the Merchant's Wife, who stood, as good Fortune would have it, at that very time watching at the Window. The Lady no sooner saw the Mask of Joy, but, without considering either the Bearer's Appearance or Gait, she came down and admitted him immediately to all the Familiarities she was used to accommodate his Master with. After all was over, the Prentice returned home, and put the Mask where he had it. A very little while after this, the Painter being come back, took out the Mask, and went to look for his Mistress. The Lady very much wondered to see the Mask again so soon; but however, with open Arms, ran to meet her Joy. She scarce opened her Mouth, however, before she unfortunately asked him the Reason of his quick Return. The Painter, on this, smelling a Rat, said not a Word more, but flung from her in a Passion, flew to his 'Prentice, and made him pay dear for the Pleasure he had tasted: Then reflecting upon the easy Condescension of the Merchant's Wife to satisfy the Desires of this Servant, he broke off all Familiarity with her. Now if the Woman had not concluded too hastily on seeing the Mask, and yielded to the Extasies of the 'Prentice, she had not lost so passionate, tho' criminal, a Lover.

The Lion's Mother observing that her Son gave Ear to *Damna* with Delight, was afraid lest the subtle Fox should by this Eloquence put a Stop to the Course of Justice. Son, therefore, said she to the Lion, my Mind forebodes to me that you will believe *Damna* innocent, and that you look upon all those that have accused him, as Liars. I never thought, continued she, that a King, who is looked upon to be the most just of Princes, could suffer himself to be thus seduced by the fair Words and glossing Insinuations of a capital Offender, who is endeavouring at nothing by all these fine Stories but to deceive you, and to escape the Rigour of the Law. So saying she rose up in a great Passion, and retired to her own Apartment; and the Lion, partly to pacify his Mother, and partly, because he begun to think *Damna* guilty, ordered him to be committed to a close Prison.

When the Room was clear, his Mother returned and addressing herself to her Son; Son, said she, think me not invidious in my Nature for thus pushing on the Fate of this Offender: 'Tis with Reluctance that I have done it, but Justice to yourself, and to the departed innocent *Cohotorbe,* require it. Guilty he unquestionably is in the highest Degree; but yet, when I recollect all Circumstances of his Life, I cannot conceive how a Person of so much Understanding came to suffer himself to be tempted to so great a Crime. Certainly, answered the King, this has been the Effect of Envy in him, that has made him commit so foul a Piece of Treachery, and is a Vice able to destroy the cunningest Minds. Envy, pursued he, is a Vice that keeps the Thoughts in a perpetual Motion, and torments us with continual Disquiet. Nay, so strangely detestable a Passion is this, that there are some who bear as Grudge even to those that do them good. This you may know by the following Example.

F A B L E VIII.

Three Envious Persons that found Money.

THREE Men once were travelling the same Road, and soon by that means became acquainted. As they were journeying on, said the eldest to the rest, Pray tell me, Fellow-travellers, why do you leave your settled Homes, to wander in foreign Countries. I have quitted my native Soil, answered one, because I could not endure the Sight of some People whom I hated worse than Death: And this Hatred of mine, I must confess, was not founded on any Injury done me by them, but arose from my own Temper, which, I own it, cannot endure to see another happy. Few Words will give you my Answer, replied the second, for the same Distemper torments my Breast, and sends me a rambling about the World. Friends, replied the eldest, then let us all embrace, for I find we are all three troubled with the same Disease. On these reciprocal Confessions they soon became acquainted, and being of the same Humour immediately closed in an Union together. One Day as they travelled through a certain deep hollow Way, they spied a Bag of Money, which some Traveller had dropt in the Road. Presently they alighted all three, and cried one to another, let us share this Money, and return home again, where we may be merry and enjoy ourselves. But this they only said in Dissimulation, for every one being unwilling that his Companion should have the least Benefit, they were truly each of them at a stand, whether it were not best to go on without meddling with the Bag, to the end that the rest might do the same; being well contented not to be happy themselves, lest another should be so also. In Conclusion, they stopt a whole Day and Night in the same Place, to consider what they should do. At the End of which Time the King of the Country riding a hunting with all his Court, the Chace led him to this Place. He rode up to the three Men, and asked them what they did with the Money that lay on the Ground? And being thus surprized, and dreading some ill Consequence if they equivocated, they all frankly told the Truth. Sir, said they we are all three turmoiled with the same Passion, which is Envy. This Passion has forced us to quit our native Country, and still keeps us Company wherever we go; and a great Act of Kindness would it be in any one, if it were possible, that he would cure us of this accursed Passion, which though we cannot but carry in our Bosoms, yet we hate and abhor. Well, said the King, I will be your Doctor; but before I can do any thing, 'tis requisite that every one of you should inform me truly in what Degree this Passion prevails over him, to the end that I may apply a Remedy in proper Proportion of Strength. My Envy, alas! said the first, had got such a Head, that I cannot endure to do good to any Man living. You are an honest Man in comparison of me, cried the second; for I am so far from doing good to another myself, that I mortally hate that any body else should do another Man good. Said the third, You both are Children in this Passion to me; neither of you possess the Quality of Envy in a Degree to be compared with me; for I not only cannot endure to oblige, nor to see any other Person obliged, but I even hate that any body should do myself a Kindness. The King was so astonished to hear them talk at this rate, that he knew not what to answer. At length, after he had considered some time, Monsters, and not Men, that ye are, said he, you deserve not that I should let you have the Money, but Punishment, if that can be, adequate to your Tempers; at the same time he commanded the bag to be taken from them, and condemned them to Punishments they justly merited. He that could not endure to do good was sent into the Desert, barefoot and without

Provision. He that could not endure to see good done to another, had his Head chopped off, because he was unworthy to live, as being one that loved nothing but Mischief. And lastly, as for him that could not endure any good to be done to himself, his Life was spared, in regard his Torment was only to himself; and he was put into a Quarter of the Kingdom where the People were of all others famous for being the best-natured, and the most addicted to the Performance of good Deeds and charitable Actions. The Goodness of these People, and the Favours they conferred upon him from Day to Day, soon became such Torment to his Soul, that he died in the utmost Anguish.

By this History, continued the Lion, you see what Envy is; that it is of all Vices the most abominable, and most to be expelled out of all human Society. Most true, replied the Mother; and 'tis for that very Reason that *Damna* ought to be put to Death, since he is attainted of so dangerous a Vice. If he be guilty, replied the Lion, he shall perish; but that I am not yet well assured of, but am resolved to be before he is condemned.

While matters were thus carrying on at Court, however, *Damna's* Wife, moved with Compassion, went to see him in his Prison, and read him this Curtain-Lecture. Did I not tell you, said she, that it behoved you too to take care of going on with the Execution of your Enterprize; and that People of Judgment and Discretion never begin a Business till they have warily considered what will be the Issue of it? A Tree is never to be planted, Spouse, continued she, before we know what Fruit it will produce. While *Kalila* was thus upbraiding *Damna*, there was in the Prison a Bear, of whom they were not aware, and who having overheard them, resolved to make use of what his Ears had furnished him withal, as Occasion should direct him.

The next Day, betimes in the Morning, the Council met again, where after every one had taken his Place, the Mother of the Lion thus began. Let us remind your Majesty, said she, that we ought no more to delay the Punishment of a capital Offender, than to hurry on the Condemnation of the Innocent; and that a King that forbears the Punishment of a Malefactor, is guilty of no less a Crime than if he had been a Confederate with him. The old Lady spoke this with much Earnestness: and the Lion considering that she spoke nothing but Reason, commanded that *Damna* should be immediately brought to his Trial. On this the Chief Justice, rising from his Seat, made the accustomed Speech on such Occasions, and desired the several Members of the Council to speak, and give their Opinion freely, boldly and honestly, in this Matter; saying withal, that it would produce three great Advantages, First, That Truth would be found out, and Justice done. Secondly, That wicked Men and Traitors would be punished. And Thirdly, That the Kingdom would be cleared of Knaves and Impostors, who, by their Artifices, troubled the Repose of it. But notwithstanding the Eloquence of the Judge, as no body then present knew the Depth of the Business, none opened their Mouths to speak. This gave *Damna* an Occasion to defend himself with so much the greater Confidence and Intrepidity: Sir, said he, rising slowly from his Seat, and making a profound Reverence to his Majesty and the Court, had I committed the Crime of which I stand accused, I might draw some Colour of Advantage from the general Silence; but I find myself so innocent, that I wait with Indifferency the End of this Assembly. Nevertheless, I must needs say this, that seeing no body had been pleased to deliver his Sentiments upon this Affair, 'tis a certain Sign that all believe me innocent. Let me not, sacred Sir, be blamed for speaking in my own Justification: I am to be excused in that, since it is lawful for every one to defend himself. Therefore, said he, pursuing his Discourse, I beseech all this illustrious Company to say in the King's Presence whatever they know concerning me; but let me caution them at the same time to have a care of affirming any thing but what is true, lest they find themselves involved in what befel the ignorant Physician; of whom, with your Majesty's Permission, I will relate the Fable.

F A B L E   IX.

The IGNORANT PHYSICIAN.

THERE was once, in a remote Part of the East, a Man who was altogether void of Knowledge and Experience, yet presumed to call himself a Physician. He was so ignorant, notwithstanding, that he knew not the Cholic from the Dropsy, nor could he distinguish Rhubarb from Bezoar. He never visited a Patient twice, for his first coming always killed him. On the other hand, there was in the same Province another Physician of that Learning and Ability, that he cured the most desperate Diseases by Virtue of the several Herbs of the Country, of which he had a perfect Knowledge. Now this learned Man became blind, and not being able to visit his Patients, at length retired into a Desart, there to live at his Ease. The ignorant Physician no sooner understood that the only Man he look'd upon with an envious Eye was retired out of the way, but he began boldly to display his Ignorance, under the Opinion of manifesting his Knowledge. One Day the King of the Country's Daughter fell sick, upon which the knowing Physician was sent for, because, that besides that he had already served the Court, People were convinced that he was much more able than he that went about to set himself up in this pompous Manner. The learned Physician being in the Princess's Chamber, and understanding the Nature of her Disease, ordered her to take a certain Pill composed of such Ingredients as he prescribed. Presently they asked him where such and such Drugs were to be had. Formerly, answered the Physician, I have seen them in such and such Boxes in the King's Treasury, but what Confusion there may have been since among those Boxes I know not. Upon this the ignorant Physician pretended that he knew the Drugs very well, and that he also knew where to find and how to make use of them. Go then, said the King, to my Treasury, and take what is requisite. Away went the ignorant Physician and fell to searching for the Box; but because many of the Boxes were alike, and for that he knew not the Drugs when he saw them, he knew not what to determine. On the whole, however, he rather chose, in the Puzzle of his Judgment, to take a Box at a venture, than to acknowledge his Ignorance. But he never considered, that they who meddle with what they understand not, are generally constrained to an early Repentance; for in the Box which he had picked out there was a most exquisite Poison, of which he made his Pills, and which he caused the Princess to take, who died immediately after: On which the King commanded the ignorant Physician to be apprehended, and condemned to Death.

This Example, pursued *Damna*, teaches us, that no Man ought to say or do a thing which he understands not. A Man may, however, perceive by your Physiognomy, said one of the Assistants, interrupting him, nothwithstanding these fine Speeches, that you are a sly Companion, one that can talk better than you can act, and therefore I pronounce, that there is little heed to be given to what you say. The Judge on this asked him that spoke last, what Proof he could produce of the Certainty of what he averred? Physiognomists, answered he, observe, that they who have their Eye-brows parted, their Left-eye bleared, and bigger than the Right, the Nose turned toward the Left-side, and who, counterfeiting your Hypocrites, cast their Eyes always toward the Ground, are generally Traitors and Sycophants; and therefore *Damna* having all these Marks, from what I know of the Art, I thought I might safely give that Character of him which I have done, without Injury to

Truth. Your art may fail you, replied *Damna*, for 'tis our Creator alone who forms us as he pleases, and gives us such a Physiognomy as he thinks fitting, and for what Purposes he best knows. And permit me to add, that, if what you say were true, and every Man carried written in his Forehead what he had in his Heart, the Wicked might certainly be distinguished from the Righteous at Sight, and there would be no need of Judges and Witnesses to determine the Disputes and Differences that arise in civil Society. In like manner it would be unjust to put some to their Oaths, and others to the Rack, to discover the Truth, because it might be evidently seen. And if the Marks you have mentioned imposed a Necessity upon those that bear them to act amiss, would it not be palpable Injustice to punish the Wicked, since they are not free in their own Actions? We must then conclude, according to this Maxim, that if I were the Cause of *Cohotorbe's* Death, I am not to be punished for it, since I am not Master of my Actions, but was forced to it by the Marks which I bear. You see, by this way of arguing therefore, that your Inferences are false. *Damna*, having thus stopt the Assistant's Mouth, no body durst adventure to say any thing more, which forced the Judge to sent him back to Prison, and left the King yet undetermined what to think of him.

Damna being returned to his Prison, was about to have sent a Messenger to *Kalila* to come to him, when a Brother Fox that was in the Room by Accident spared him that Trouble, by informing him of *Kalila's* Death, who died the Day before for Grief to see her Husband intangled in such an unfortunate Affair.

The News of *Kalila's* Death touched *Damna* so to the quick, that, like one who cared not to live any longer, he seemed to be altogether comfortless. Upon which the Fox endeavoured to chear him up, telling him, that if he had lost a dear and loving Wife, he might, however, if he pleased to try him, find him a zealous and a faithful Friend. *Damna*, on this, knowing he had no Friend left that he could trust, and for that the Fox so frankly proffered him his Service, accepted his Kindness, I beseech you then, said *Damna*, go to the Court, and give me a faithful Account of what People say of me: This is the first Proof of Friendship which I desire of you.

Most willingly, answered the Fox; and immediately taking

his Leave, he went to the Court, to see what Observations he could make.

The next Morning, by Break of Day, the Lion's Mother went to her Son, and asked him what he had determined to do with *Damna*? He is still in Prison, answered the King, and I can find nothing proved upon him yet, nor know I what to do about him. What a deal of Difficulty is here, replied the Mother, to condemn a Traitor and a Villain, who deserves more Punishments than you can inflict; and yet I am afraid, when all's done, will escape by his Dexterity and Cunning. I cannot blame you for being discontented with these Delays, replied the King, for I also am so, but know not how to help myself; and if you please to be present at his next Examination yourself, I will order it immediately, and you shall see what will be resolved upon. Which said, he ordered *Damna* to be sent for, that the Business might be brought to a Conclusion. The King's Orders were obeyed, and the Prisoner being brought to the Bar, the Chief Justice put the same Question as the Day before, Whether any body had any thing to say against *Damna*? But no body said a Word; which *Damna* observing, I am glad to see, said he, that in your Majesty's Court there is not a single Villain; few sovereign Princes can say as much: But here is Proof of the Truth of it before us, in that there is no body here who will bear false Witness, though it be wished by every one that something were said: And in other Courts 'twere well if the same Honour and Honesty were kept up. And let me advise all from the Villany of bearing false Witness, for their own Sakes, and for fear of exposing themselves to the Punishment which the Falconer once incurred, for having given a false Testimony.

F A B L E X.

The virtuous WOMAN *and the young* FALCONER.

A Very honest and rich Merchant had once a Wife no less modest than beautiful: Among the rest of his Servants this Merchant had also a young Lad that was very vicious, but he could not find in his Heart to put him away, because he was a good Falconer, and the Merchant greatly delighted in this Diversion. Now in regard it is the Custom of the Eastern People to keep their Women very private, this Lad for a long time had never seen his Mistress. But having viewed her one Day by Accident, he became passionately in love with her. In despight of all Danger he ventured to court her Affection, by means of a Female Friend, whom he with much Trouble got over to his Interest. But both he and she lost all their Labour, for they had to do with a truly virtuous Woman. At length, despairing to prosper in his Amours, he changed his Love into Hatred, and meditated a most bloody Revenge. To this Effect he cunningly went and bought two Parrots; one of which he taught to pronounce these Words, *I saw my Mistress in Bed with the Falconer:* and the other, *For my part, I say nothing.* In a little time after these Birds had learned their Lesson, the Merchant having invited his

Friends to a great Feast, when every body was seated at the Table, these Parrots began to repeat their Lesson. Now the Falconer had taught these Parrots to speak the Words in his own Country Language, which was different from that of the Place, and because the Master, Mistress, nor any of the Servants understood what they meant, no body minded their repeating them. But this was not the Case now, for some of the Guests, who happened to be the Falconer's Countrymen, no sooner heard the Parrots, but they forbore eating, and stared with the utmost Amazement one at another. The Merchant, astonished at this, asked them the Reason. Do you not understand, answered the Guests, what these Birds say? No, replied the Merchant. Why they say, said the Guest that spoke first, that your Falconer has made you a Cuckold. The Merchant was astonished and confounded at these Words, and begg'd Pardon of his Friends for having invited them to a Place where so much Uncleanness had been committed. The Falconer also, the more to exasperate his Master against his Wife, confessed the Fact, and said that it was true. Which put the Husband into so great a Rage, that he ordered his Wife to be put to death.

When they that were ordered to execute her Husband's Command came to her, and with a great Sorrow acquainted her with their Business, she told them that she was ready to suffer any Punishment which her Husband, who was he Lord and sovereign Master, thought fit to inflict upon her; but that as she was innocent of the Crime she was accused of, she could have wished he would, for the sake of his own future Peace, have heard her first; for that if her Innocence should afterwards come to be known, his Repentance would be then too late. This being reported to her Husband, he sent for her into a little Closet, whither he ordered he to come veil'd, and bid her justify herself, if she could. The Parrots, said he, are not rational Creatures, and therefore cannot be accused either of Imposture or Bribery: How then will you justify yourself against what they accuse you of?

You are bound, my dear Lord, in Duty and Honour, answered the Wife, to be well assured of the Truth, in a Case of this kind, before you condemn me to death; and there is an easy way by which you may know it: Ask those Gentlemen whether they observe any Variety of Relation in these Parrots Speech, or whether they only repeat the fame set Words over and over again. If they only repeat the same Words, be assured they speak not of Knowledge or Design, and have only been taught to repeat them, and that it is a Device made use of by your Servant, to provoke your undeserved Anger against me, because he could not obtain those Favours from me which he desired, and which he had long sollicited, though I have been so charitable to his Youth as not to accuse him to you of it. If it be thus, let the Weight of your Anger fall on him: If otherwise, let me perish. The Merchant judging, by her prudent Advice, that she might not be guilty, went to his Guests, carried them the Parrots, and desired them to stay with him, and diligently observed for two or three Days, whether the Birds spoke any thing else beside what they had heard; which the Guests accordingly did. The Result of this was, that they found the Parrots always in the same Lesson, of which they faithfully informed the Merchant, who then acknowledged the Innocence of his Wife, and was sensible of the Malice of his Servant. The Falconer was now sent for, and instantly appeared with his Hawk upon his Fist; to whom the Wife, Villain, said she, how didst thou dare to accuse me of so foul a Crime? Because you were guilty, answered the Servant. But he had no sooner uttered the Words, than the Hawk upon his Fist flew in his Face and tore out his Eyes; and the Husband acknowledged the Injustice he was like to have been guilty of, and on his Knees implored his Wife's Pardon.

This Example, said *Damna*, pursuing his Discourse, instructs us how hainous a thing it is to bear false Witness; and that it always turns to our Shame and Confusion. Happy therefore is your Majesty, who have no Subject in your whole Dominions wicked enough to be guilty of it. After *Damna* had done speaking, the Lion looking upon his Mother, asked her Opinion. I find, answered she, that you have a Kindess for this most cunning Villain; but believe me he will, if you pardon him, cause nothing but Faction and Disorder in your Court. I beseech you, replied the Lion, to tell me who has so strongly prepossessed you against *Damna*. It is but too true, replied the Queen-Mother, that he has committed the Crime that is laid to his Charge. I know him to be guilty, but I shall not now discover the Person who intrusted me with this Secret. However, I will go to him, and ask him whether he will be willing that I should bring to him in for a Witness: And so saying, she went home immediately, and sent for the Leopard.

When he was come: This Villain whom you have accused to me, said she, will escape the Hands of Justice, unless you appear yourself against him. Go therefore, continued she, at my Request, and boldly declare what thou knowest concerning *Damna*. Fear no Danger in so honest a Cause, for no Ill shall befall thee. Madam, answered the Leopard, You know that I could wish to be excused from this, but you also know that I am ready to sacrifice my Life to your Majesty's Commands; dispose of me, therefore, as you please; I am ready to go wherever you command. With that she carried the Leopard to the King; to whom, Sir, said she, here is an undeniable Witness which I have to produce against *Damna*. Then the Lion, addressing himself to the Leopard, asked him what Proof he had of the Delinquent's Treason? Sir, answered the Leopard, I was willing to conceal this Truth, on purpose, for some time, to see what Reasons the cunning Traitor would bring to justify himself; but now 'tis time your Majesty knew all. On this the Leopard made a long Recital of what had passed between *Kalila* and her Husband: Which Deposition being made in the hearing of several Beasts, was soon divulged far and near, and presently afterwards confirm'd by a second Testimony, which was the Bear's, of whom I made mention before, After this the Delinquent was ask'd what he had now to say for himself; but he had not a Word to answer. This at length determined the Lion to sentence, that *Damna*, as a Traitor, should be shut up between four Walls, and there starved to Death.

These Chapters, concluded *Pilpay*, may it please your Majesty, are Lessons to Deceivers and Sycophants, that they ought to reform their Manners, and I think have sufficiently made it appear, that Slanderers and Railers generally come to an unfortunate End; besides, that while they live they render themselves odious to all human Society. He that plants Thorns, must never expect to gather Roses.

C H A P. IV.

How we ought to make Choice of FRIENDS, *and what Advantage may be reaped from their Conversation.*

YOU have now told me, said the King, to my infinite Satisfaction, the Story of a Knave, who, under the false Appearances of Friendship, occasioned the Death of an innocent Person. I desire you next to inform me what Benefit may be made of honest Men and real Friends in civil Life. Your Majesty, answer'd the *Bramin*, is to know that honest Men esteem and value nothing so much in this World as a real Friend. Such a one is as it were another self, to whom we impart our most sercret Thoughts, who partakes of our Joy, and comforts us in our Affliction: Add to this, that his Company is an everlasting Pleasure to us. But nothing can, perhaps, give your Majesty a clearer or nobler Idea of the Pleasures of a reciprocal Friendship than the following Fable:

F A B L E I.

The RAVEN, *the* RAT, *and the* PIGEONS.

NEAR adjoining to *Odorna* there was once a most delightful Place, which was extremely full of Wild-fowl, and was therefore much frequented by the Sportsmen and Fowlers. A Raven one Day accidentally espied in this Place, at the Foot of a Tree, on the Top of which she had built her Nest, a certain Fowler with a Net in his Hand. The poor Raven was afraid at first, imagining it was herself that the Fowler aimed at; but her Fears ceased when she observed the Motions of the Person, who, after he had spread his Net upon the Ground, and scattered some Corn about it to allure the Birds, went and hid himself behind a Hedge, where he was no sooner laid down, but a flock of Pigeons threw themselves upon the Corn, without hearkening to their Chieftain, who would fain have hindered them, telling them, that they were not so rashly to abandon themselves to their Passions. This prudent Leader, who was an old Pigeon, called *Montivaga,* perceiving them so obstinate, had many times a Desire to separate himself from them; but Fate, that imperiously controuls all living Creatures, constrained him to follow the Fortune of the rest, so that he alighted upon the Ground with his Companions. It was not long after this before they all saw themselves under the Net, and just ready to fall into the Fowler's Hands. Well, said *Montivaga* on this, mournfully, to them, What think you now, will you believe me another time, if it be possible that you may get away from this Destruction? I see, continued he, perceiving how they fluttered to get loose, that every one of you minds his own Safety only, never regarding what becomes of his Companions; and, let me tell you, that this is not only an ungratful, but foolish, way of acting; we ought to make it our Business to help one another, and it may be so charitable an Action may save us all; let us all together strive to break the Net. On this they all obeyed *Montivaga,* and so well bestirred themselves, that they tore the Net up from the Ground, and carried it up with them into the Air. The Fowler on this, vexed to lose so fair a Prey, followed the Pigeons, in hopes that the Weight of the Net would tire them.

In the mean-time the Raven observing all this, said to herself, This is a very pleasant Adventure, I am resolved to see the Issue of it; and accordingly she took wing and followed them. *Montivaga* observing that the Fowler was resolved to pursue them, This Man, said he to his Companions, will never give over pursuing us, till he has lost Sight of us; therefore, to prevent our Destruction, let us bend our Flight to some thick Wood, or some ruined Castle, to the end that when we are protected by some Forest or thick Wall, Despair may force him to retire. This Expedient had the desired Success; for, having secured themselves among the Boughs of a thick Forest, where the Fowler lost sight of them, he returned home, full sorely afflicted for the Loss of his Game and his Net to boot.

As for the Raven, she followed them still, out of Curiosity to know how they got out of the Net, that she might make use of the same Secret upon the like Occasion.

The Pigeons, thus quit of the Fowler, were overjoyed; however, they were still troubled with the Intanglements of the Net, which they could not get rid of: But *Montivaga* who was fertile in Inventions, soon found a way for that. We must address ourselves, said he, to some intimate Friend, who, setting aside all treacherous and By-ends, will go faithfully to work for our Deliverance. I know a Rat, continued he, that lives not far from hence, a faithful

Friend of mine, whose Name is *Zirac;* he, I know, will gnaw the Net, and set us at Libery. The Pigeons, who desired nothing more, all intreated to fly to this Friend; and soon after they arrived at the Rat's Hole, who came forth upon the fluttering of their Wings; and astonished and surprized to see *Montivaga* so intangled in the Net, O! my dear Friend, said he, how came you into this Condition? To whom *Montivaga* replied, I desire you, my most faithful Friend, first of all to disengage my Companions. But *Zirac,* more troubled to see his Friend bound than for all the rest, would needs pay his Respects to him first; but *Montivaga* cried out, I conjure you once more, by our sacred Friendship, to set my Companions at Libery before me; for, that besides being their Chieftain, I ought to take care for them in the first Place, I am afraid the Pains thou wilt take to unbind me, will slacken thy good Offices to the rest; whereas, the Friendship thou hast for me will excite thee to hasten their Deliverance, that thou may'st be sooner in a Condition to give me my Freedom. The Rat admiring the Solidity of these Arguments, applauded *Montivaga's* Generosity, and fell to unloosen the Strangers; which was soon done, and then he performed the same kind Office for his Friend.

Montivaga, thus at Liberty, together with his Companions, took leave of *Zirac,* returning him a thousand Thanks for his Kindness. And when they were gone, the Rat returned to his Hole.

The Raven, having observed all this, had a great Desire to be aquainted with *Zirac.* To which end he went to his Hole, and called him by his Name. *Zirac,* frighted to hear a strange Voice, asked who he was? To which the Raven answered, It is a Raven who has some Business of Importance to impart to thee. What Business, replied the Rat, can you and I have together? We are Enemies. Then the Raven told him, he desired to list himself in the Number of the Rat's Acquaintance, whom he knew to be so sincere a Friend. I beseech you, answered *Zirac* find out some other Creature, whose Friendship agrees better with your Disposition. You lose your time in endeavouring to persuade me to such an incompatible Reconciliation. Never stand · upon Incompatibilities, said the Raven, but do a generous Action, by affording an innocent Person your Friendship and Acquaintance, when he desires it at your Hands. You may talk to me of Generosity till your Lungs ache, replied *Zirac,* I know your Tricks too well: In a Word, we are Creatures of so different Species, that we can never be either Friends or Acquaintance. The Example which I remember of the Partridge, that over-hastily granted her Friendship to a Falcon, is sufficient Warning to make me wiser.

F A B L E II.

The PARTRIDGE *and the* FALCON.

A PARTRIDGE, said *Zirac*, keeping close in his Hole, but very obligingly pursuing his Discourse, was promenading at the Foot of a Hill, and turning her Throat in her coarse way, so delightfully, that a Falcon flying that way, and hearing her Voice, came towards her, and very civilly was going to ask her Acquaintance. Nobody, said he to himself, can live without a Friend; and it is the saying of the Wife, that they who want Friends, labour under perpetual Sickness. With these Thoughts he would fain have accosted the Partridge; but she perceiving him, escaped into a Hole, all over in a cold Sweat for Fear. The Falcon followed her, and presenting himself at the Foot of the Hole, My dear Partridge, said he, I own that I never had any great Kindness hitherto for you, because I did not know your Merit; but since my good Fortune now has made me acquainted with your merry Note, be pleased to give me leave to speak with you, that I may offer you my Friendship, and that I may beg of you to grant me yours. Tyrant, answered the Partridge, let me alone, and labour not in vain to reconcile Fire and Water. Most amiable Partridge, replied the Falcon, banish these idle Fears, and be convinced that I love you, and desire that we may enter into a Familiarity together: Had I any other Design, I would not trouble myself to court you with such soft Language out of your Hole. Believe me, I have such good Pounces, that I would have seized a dozen other Partridges in the time that I have been courting your Affection: I am sure you will have Reasons enough to be glad of my Friendship; first, because no other Falcon shall do any Harm, while you are under my Protection; secondly, because that being in my Nest, you will be honoured by the World; and, lastly, I will procure you a Male to keep you Company, and give you all the Delights of Love and a young Progeny. It is impossible for me to think that you can have so much Kindness to me, replied the Partridge; but indeed should this be true, I ought not to accept your Próposal; for you being the Prince of Birds, and of the greatest Strength, and I a poor weak Partridge, whenever I shall do any thing that displeases you, you will not fail to tear me to Pieces. No, no, said the Falcon, set your Heart at rest for that; the Faults that Friends commit are easily pardoned. Much other Discourse of this kind passed between them, and many Doubts were started and answered to Satisfaction, so that at length the Falcon testified such an extraodinary Friendship for the Partridge, that she could no longer refuse coming out of her Hole. And no sooner was she come forth, but the Falcon tenderly embraced her, and carried her to his Nest, where, for two or three Days he made it his whole Business to divert her. The Partridge, overjoyed to see herself so caressed, gave her Tongue more Liberty than she had done before, and talked much of the Cruelty and savage Temper of the Birds of Prey. This began to offend the Falcon, though, for the present, he dissembled it. One Day, however, he unfortunately fell ill, which hindered him from going abroad in search of Prey, so that he grew hungry, and wanting Victuals, he soon became melancholy, morose and churlish. His being out of Humour quickly alarmed the Partridge, who kept herself, very prudently, close in a Corner with a very modest Countenance. But the Falcon, soon after, no longer able to endure the Importunities of his Stomach, resolved to pick a Quarrel with the poor Partridge. To which purpose, It is not fitting, said he, that you should lye lurking there in the Shade, while all the

World is exposed to the Heat of the Sun. The Partridge, trembling every Joint of her, replied, King of the Birds, it is now Night, all the World is in the Shade as well as I, not do I know what Sun you mean. Insolent Baggage, replied the Falcon, then you will make me either a liar or mad: And so saying, he fell upon her and tore her to Pieces.

Do not believe, pursued the Rat, that upon the Faith of your Promises, I will lay myself at your Mercy. Recollect yourself, answered the Raven, and consider that it is not worth my while to fool my Stomach with such a diminutive Body as thine, it is therefore with no such Intent I am talking with thee, but I know thy Friendship may be beneficial to me; scruple not therefore to grant me this Favour. The Sages of old, replied the Rat, admonish us to take care of being deluded by the fair Words of our Enemies, as was a certain unfortunate Man, whose Story, if you please, I will relate to you.

F A B L E III.

The MAN *and the* ADDER.

A MAN mounted upon a Camel, once rode into a Thicket, and went to rest himself in that Part of it, from whence a Caravan was just departed, and where the People having left a Fire, some Sparks of it being driven by the Wind had set a Bush, wherein lay an Adder, all in a Flame. The Fire environed the Adder in such a manner, that he knew not how to escape, and was just giving himself over to Destruction, when he perceived the Man already mentioned, and with a thousand mournful Conjurations, begged of him to save his Life. The Man, on this, being naturally compassionate, said to himself, It is true, these Creatures are Enemies to Mankind; however, good Actions are of great Value, even of the very greatest when done to our Enemies, and whoever sows the Seed of good Works, shall reap the Fruit of Blessings. After he had made this Reflexion, he took a Sack, and tying it to the End of his Lance, reached it over the Flame to the Adder, who flung himself into it; and when he was safe in, the Traveller pulled back the Bag, and gave the Adder leave to come forth, telling him he might go about his Business, but hoped he would have the Gratitude to make him a Promise, never to do any more Harm to Men, since a Man had done him so great a piece of Service. To this the ungrateful Creature answered, You much mistake both yourself and me; think not that I intend to be gone so calmly; no, my Design is first to leave thee a parting Blessing, and throw my Venom upon thee and they Camel. Monster of Ingratitude, replied the Traveller, desist a Moment at least, and tell me whether it be lawful to recompense Good with Evil? No, replied the Adder, it certainly is not, but in acting in that manner, I shall do no more than what yourselves do every day; that is to say, retaliate good Deeds with wicked Actions, and requite Benefits with Ingratitude. You cannot prove this slanderous and wicked Aspersion, replied the Traveller; nay, I will venture to say, that if you can shew me any one other Creature in the World, that is of your Opinion, I will consent to whatever Punishment you think fit to inflict on me for the Faults of my Fellow-Creatures. I agree to this willingly, answered the Adder; and at the same time spying a Cow, let us propound our Question, said he, to this Creature before us, and we shall see what Answer she will make. The Man consented, and so both of them accosting the Cow, the Adder put the Question to her, how a good Turn was to be requited? By its Contrary, replied the Cow, if you mean according to the Custom of Men; and this I know by sad Experience. I belong, said she, to a Man, to whom I have long several ways extremely beneficial: I have been used to bring him Calf every Year, and to supply his House with Milk, Butter, and Cheese; but now I am grown old, and no longer in a Condition to serve him as formerly I did, he has put in this Pasture to fat me, with a Design to sell me to a Butcher, who is to cut my Throat, and he and his Friends are to eat my Flesh: And is not a requiting Good with Evil? On this the Adder taking upon him to speak, said to the Man, What say you now, are not your own Customs a sufficient Warrant for me to treat you as I intend to do? The Traveller, not a little confounded at this ill timed Story, was cunning enough, however, to answer, This is a particular Case only, and give me leave to say, one Witness is not sufficient to convict me; therefore pray let me have another. With all my Heart, replied the Adder; let us address ourselves to this Tree that stands here before us. The Tree having heard the Subject of their Dispute, gave his Opinion in the following Words: Among Men Benefits are never requited but with ungrateful Actions. I protect Travellers from the Heat of the Sun, and yield them Fruit to eat, and a delightful Liquor to drink; nevertheless, forgetting the Delight and Benefit of my Shade, they barbarously cut down my Branches to make Sticks and Handles for Hatchets, and saw my Body to make Planks and Rafters. Is not this requiting Good with Evil? The Adder, on this, looking upon the Traveller, asked if he was satisfied? But he was in such Confusion, that he knew not what to answer. However, in hopes to free himself from the Danger that threatened him, said to the Adder, I desire only one Favour more; let us be judged by the next Beast we meet; give me but that Satisfaction, it is all I crave; you know Life is sweet; suffer me therefore to beg for the Means of continuing it. While they were thus parleying together, a Fox passing by, was stopped by the Adder, who conjured him to put an end to their Controversy. The Fox, upon this, desiring to know the Subject to their Dispute; said the Traveller, I have done this Adder a signal Piece of Service, and he would sain persuade me that, for my Reward, he ought to do me a Mischief. If he means to act by you as you Men do by others, he speaks nothing but what is true, replied the Fox; but, that I may be better able to judge between you, let me understand what Service it is that you have done him? The Traveller was very glad of this Opportunity of speaking for himself, and recounted the whole Affair to him; he told him after what manner he had rescued him out of the Flames, with that little Sack which he shewed him. How! said the Fox, laughing out right, would you pretend to make me believe that so large an Adder as this could get into such a little Sack? 'tis impossible. Both the Man and the Adder, on this, assured him of the Truth of that Part of the Story; but the Fox positively refused to believe it. At length, said he, Words will never convince me of this monstrous Improbability; but if the Adder will go into it again, to convince me of the Truth of what you say, I shall then be able to judge of the rest of this Affair. That I will do most willingly, replied the Adder; and, at the same Time, put himself into the Sack. Then, said the Fox, to the Traveller, now you are the Master of your Enemy's Life; and, I believe, you need not be long in resolving what Treatment such a Monster of Ingratitude deserves of you. With that the Traveller tied up the Mouth of the Sack, and, with a great Stone, never left off beating it till he had pounded the Adder to Death; and, by that Means, put an end to his Fears, and the Dispute, at once.

This Fable, pursued the Rat, informs us, that there is no trusting to the fair Words of an Enemy, for fear of falling into the like Misfortunes. You say very true, replied the Raven, in all this; but what I have to answer to it is, that we ought to understand how to distinguish Friends from Enemies: And, when you have learnt that Art, you will know I am no terrible or treacherous Foe, but a sincere and hearty Friend; for I protest to thee, in a most solemn Manner, that what I have seen thee do for thy Friend the Pigeon, and his Companions, has taken such root in me, that I cannot live without an Acquaintance with thee; and I swear I will not depart from hence till thou hast granted me thy Friendship. *Zirac* perceiving, at length, that the Raven really dealt frankly and cordially with him, replied, I am happy to find that you are sincere in all this; pardon my Fears, and now hear me acknowledge, that I think 'tis an Honour for me to wear the Title of thy Friend; and, if I have so long withstood thy Importunities, it was only to try thee, and to shew thee that I want neither Wit nor Policy, that thou may'st know hereafter how far I may be able to serve thee. And so saying, he came forward; but even now he did not venture fairly out, but stops at the Entrance of his Hole. Why dost thou not come boldly forth? demanded the Raven. It is because thou art not yet assured of my Affection? That's not the Reason, answered the Rat, but I am afraid of thy Companions upon the Trees. Set thy Heart at rest for that, replied the Raven, they shall respect thee as their Friend: For 'tis a Custom among us, that, when one of us enters into a League of Friendship with a Creature of another Species, we all esteem and love that Creature. The Rat, upon the Faith of these Words, came out to the Raven, who caressed him with extraordinary Demonstrations of Friendship; swearing to him in inviolable Amity, and requesting him to go and live with him near the Habitation of a certain neighbouring Tortoise, of whom he gave a very noble Character. Command me henceforward in all Things, replied *Zirac*, for I have so great a Inclination for you, that from henceforward I will for ever follow you as your Shadow; and, to tell you the Truth, this is not the proper

Place of my Residence; I was only compelled, some Time since, to take Sanctuary in this Hole, by reason of an Accident, of which I would give you the Relation, if I thought it might not be offensive to you. My dear Friend, replied the Raven, can you have any such Fears? or rather are you not convinced that I share in all your Concerns? but the Tortoise, added he, whose Friendship is a very considerable Acquisition, which you cannot fail of, will be no less glad to hear the Recital of your Adventures: Come, therefore, away with me to her, continued he; and, at the same Time, he took the Rat in his Bill, and carred him to the Tortoise's Dwelling, to whom he related what he had seen *Zirac* do. She congratulated the Raven for having acquired so perfect a Friend, and caressed the Rat at a very high Rate; who, for his Part, was too much a Courtier not to testify how sensible he was of all her Civilities. After many Compliments on all Sides, they went all three to walk by the Banks of a purling Rivulet; and having made choice of a Place somewhat distant from the Highway, the Raven desired *Zirac* there to relate his Adventures, which he did in the following Manner.

F A B L E IV.

The Adventures of ZIRAC.

I was born, said *Zirac*, and lived many Years, in the City of *India* called *Marout*, where I made choice of a Place to reside in that seemed to be the Habitation of Silence itself, that I might live without Disturbance. Here I enjoyed long the greatest Felicity, and tasted the Sweets of a quiet Life, in Company of some other Rats, honest Creatures, of my own Humour. There was also in our Neighbourhood, I must inform you, a certain Dervice, who every Day remained idle in his Habitation while his Companion went a begging. He constantly, however, eat a Part of what the other brought home, and kept the Remainder for his Supper. But, when he set down to his second Meal, he never found his Dish in the same Condition that he left it. For, while he was in his Garden, I always filled my Belly, and constantly called my Companions to partake with me, who were no less mindful of their Duty to Nature than myself. The Dervise, on this constantly finding his Pittance diminished, flew out at length into a great Rage, and looked into his Books for some Receipt, or some Engine to apprehend us; but all that nothing availed him; I was still more cunning than he. One unfortunate Day, however, one of his Friends, who had been a long Journey, entered into his Cell to visit him; and, after they had dined, they fell into a Discourse concerning Travel. This Dervise, our good Purveyor, among other Things, asked his Friend what he had seen, that was most rare and curious, in his Travels. To whom the Traveller began to recount what he had observed most worthy Remark; but, as he was studying to give him a Description of the most delightful Places through which he had passed, the Dervise still interrupted him from Time to Time, with the Noise which he made, clapping his Hands one against the other, and stamping with his Foot against the Ground, to fright us away: For, indeed, we made frequent Sallies upon his Provision, never regarding his Presence nor his Company. At length, the Traveller taking it in dudgeon that the Dervise gave so little Ear to him, told him, in downright Terms, that he did ill to detain him there, to trouble him with telling Stories he did not attend to, and make a Fool of him. Heaven forbid! replied the Dervise altogether surprised, that I should make a Fool of a Person of your Merit: I beg your Pardon for interrupting you, but there is in this Place a Nest of Rats that will eat me up to the very Ears before they have done; and there is one above the rest so bold, that he even has the Impudence to come and bite me by the Toes as I lie asleep, and I know not now to catch the felonious Devil. The Traveller, on this, was satisfied with the Dervise's Excuses; and replied, Certainly there is some Mystery in this: This Accident brings to my Mind a remarkable Story, which I will relate to you, provided you will hearken to me with a little better Attention.

F A B L E V.

A Husband *and his* Wife.

One Day, continued the Traveller, as I was on my Journey, the bad Weather constrained me to stop at a Town, where I had several Acquaintance of different Ranks; and, being unable to proceed on my Journey for the Continuance of the Rain, I went to lodge at one of my Friends, who received me very civilly. After Supper, he put me to Bed in a Chamber that was parted from his own by a very thin Wainscot, so that, in despight of my Ears, I heard all his private Conversation with his Wife. To-morrow, said he, I intend to invite the principal Burghers of the Town, to divert my Friend, who has done me the Honour to come and see me. You have not sufficient wherewithal to support your Family, answered his Wife, and yet you talk of being a great Expences: Rather think of sparing that little you have for the Good of your Children, and let Feasting alone. This is a Man of great Religion and Piety, replied the Husband, and I ought to testify my Joy on seeing him, and to give my other Friends an Opportunity of hearing his pious Conversation; nor be you in Care for the small Expense that will attend this. The Providence of God is very great, and we ought not to take too much Care for To-morrow, left what befel the Wolf befal us.

FABLE VI.

The HUNTER *and the* WOLF.

ONE Day, continued the Husband, a great Hunter
returning from the Chace of a Deer, which he had killed,
unexpectedly espied a wild Boar coming out of a Wood, and
making directly towards him. Very good, cried the Hunter,
this Beast comes very good-naturedly, he will not a little
augment my Provision. With that he bent his Bow, and let
fly his Arrow with so good an Aim, that he wounded the
Boar to Death. Such, however, are the unforeseen Events
that attend too covetous a Care for the Necessaries of Life,
that this fair Beginning was but a Prelude to a very fatal
Catastrophe: For the Beast, feeling himself wounded, ran
with so much Fury at the Hunter, that he ript up his Belly
with his Tusks in such a manner, that they both fell dead
upon the Place.

At the very Moment when this happened, there passed by
a Wolf half-famished, who seeling so much Victuals lying
upon the Ground, was in an Extacy of Joy. However, said he
to himself, I must not be prodigal of all this good Food; but
it behoves me to husband my good Fortune, to make my
Provision hold out the longer. Being very hungry, however,

he very prudently resolved to fill his Belly first, and make his Store for future afterwards. Not willing, however, to waste any Part of his Treasure, he was for eating his Meat, and, if possible, having it too; he therefore resolved to fill his Belly with what was least delicate, and accordingly began with the String of the Bow, which was made of Gut; but he had no sooner snapt the String, than the Bow, which was highly bent, gave him such a terrible Thump upon the Breast, that he fell stone dead upon the other Bodies.

This Fable, said the Husband, pursuing his Discourse, instructs us that we ought not to be too greedily covetous. Nay, said the Wife. if this be the Effect of saving, e'en invite whom you please To-morrow.

The Company was accordingly invited; but the next Day, as the Wife was getting Dinner ready, and making a Sort of Sauce with Honey, she saw a Rat fall into the Honey-pot, which turned her Stomach, and stopped the making of that Part of the Entertainment. Unwilling, therefore, to make use of the Honey, she carried it to the Market, and, when she parted with it, took Pitch in Exchange. I was then, by Accident, by her, and asked her why she made such a disadvantageous Exchange for her Honey? Because, said she in my Ear, 'tis not worth so much to me as the Pitch. Then I presently perceived there was some Mystery in the Affair, which was beyond my Comprehension. 'Tis the same with this Rat: He would never be so bold, had he not some Reason for it which we are ignorant of. The Rats, continued he, in this Part of the World are a cunning, covetous, and proud Generation; they heap Money as much as the Misers of our own Species; and when one of them is possessed of a considerable Sum, he becomes a Prince among them, and has his Set of Comrades, who would die to serve him, as they live by him, for he disburses Money for their Purchases of Food, &c, of one another, and they live his Slaves in perfect Idleness. And for my part, I am apt to believe that this is the Case with this impudent Rat: that he had a Number of Slaves of his own Species at Command, to defend and uphold him in his audacious Tricks, and that there is Money hidden in his Hole.

The Dervise no sooner heard the Traveller talk of Money, but he took a Hatchet, and so bestirred himself, that, having cleft the Wall, he soon discovered my Treasure, to the Value of a thousand Deniers in Gold, which I had heaped together

with great Labour and Toil. These had long been my whole
Pleasure; I told them every Day; I took Delight to handle
them and tumble upon them, placing all my Happiness in
that Exercise. But to return to the Story. When the Gold
tumbled out, Very good, said the Traveller, had I not
reason to attribute the Insolence of these Rats to some
unknown Cause?

I leave you to judge in what a desperate Condition I was,
when I saw my Habitation ransacked after this Manner. I
resolved on this to change my Lodging; but all my
Companions lent me; so that I had a thorough Experience
of the Truth of the Proverb, *No Money, no Friend*. Friends,
now-a-days, love us no longer than our Friendship turns to
their Advantage. I have heard, among the Men, that one
Day a wealthy and a witty Man was asked, How many
Friends he had? As for Friends a-la-mode, said he, I have as
many as I have Crowns; but as for real Friends, Must stay till
I come to be in want, and then I shall know.

While I was pondering, however, upon the Accident that
had befallen me, I saw a Rat pass along, who had been
heretofore used to profess himself to much devoted to my
Service, that you would have thought he could not have
lived a Moment out of my Company. I called to him, and
asked him, Why he shunned me like the rest? Thinkest
thou, said the ungrateful and impudent Villain, that we are
such Fools to serve thee for nothing? When thoe wert rich,
we were thy Servants; but, now thou art poor, believe me,
we will not be the Companions of thy Poverty. Alas! thou
ought'st not to despite the Poor, said I, because they are
the beloved of Providence. 'Tis very true, answered he; but
not such poor as thou art; for Providence takes care of those
among Men who have, for the sake of Religion, forsaken the
World; not those whom the World had fortaken. Miserably
angry was I with myself for my former Generosities to such
a Wretch; but I could not tell what to answer to such a
cutting Expression. I said, however, notwithstanding my
Misfortunes, with the Dervise, to see how he would dispose
of the Money he had taken from me, and I observed that he
gave one half to his Friend, and that each of them laid their
Shares under their Pillows. On seeing this, an immediate
Thought came into my Mind to go and regain this Money.
To this Purpose I stole softly to the Dervise's Bed-side, and
was just going to carry back my Treasure; but unfortunately

his Friend, who, unperceived by me, observed all my
Actions, threw his Bed-staff at me so good a Will, that he
had almost broke my Foot, which obliged me to recover my
Hole with all the Speed I could, though not without some
Difficulty. About an Hour after, I crept out again, believing,
by this time, the Traveller might be asleep also. But he was
too diligent a Centinel, and too much afraid of losing his
good Fortune. However, I plucked up a good Heart, went
forward, and was already got to the Dervise's Bed's-head,
when my Rashness had like to have cost me my Life. For the
Traveller gave me a second Blow upon the Head, that
stunned me in such a manner, that I could hardly find my
Hole again. At the same Instant he also threw his Bed-staff
at me a third time; but missing me, I recovered my
Sanctuary, where I was no sooner sat down in Safety, but I
protested never more to pursue the Recovery of a Thing
which had cost me so much Pains and Jeopardy. In
pursuance of this Resolution, I left the Dervise's
Habitation, and retired to that Place where you saw me with
the Pigeon. The Tortoise was extremely well pleased with
the Recital of the Rat's Adventures, and at the same time
embracing him, You have done well, said she, to quit the
World, and the Intrigues of it, since they afford us no
perfect Satisfaction. All those who are turmoiled with
Avarice and Ambition do but labour their own Ruin, like a
certain Cat, which I once knew, whose Adventures you will
not be displeased to hear.

F A B L E VII.

The RAVENOUS CAT.

A CERTAIN Person, whom I have often seen, continued the Tortoise, bred up a Cat very frugally in his own House. He gave her enough to suffice Nature, though nothing superfluous; and she might, if she pleased, have lived very happily with him; but she was very ravenous, and not content with her ordinary Food, hunted about in every Corner for more. One Day, passing by a Dove-house, she saw some young Pigeons, that were hardly fledged, and presently her Teeth watered for a Taste of those delicate Viands. With this Resolution up she boldly mounted into the Dove-house, never minding whether the Master were there or no, and was presently, with great Joy, preparing to satisfy her voluptuous Desires. But the Master of the Place no sooner saw the Epicure of a Cat enter, but he shut up the Doors, and stopped all the Holes at which it was possible for her to get out again, and so bestirred himself, that he caught the felonious Baggage, and hanged her up at the Corner of the Pigeon-house. Soon after this, the Owner of the Cat passing that way, and seeing his Cat hanged, Unfortunate Greedy-gut, said he, hadst thou been contented with thy meaner Food, thou hadst not been now in this Condition! Thus, continued he, moralizing on the Spectacle, infatiable Gluttons are the Procurers of their own untimely Ends. Alas! the Felicities of this World are uncertain, and of no Continuance. Wife Men, I well remember, say, there is no reliance upon these six things, nor any thing of Fidelity to be expected from them:

1. From a Cloud; for it disperses in an Instant.

2. From feigned Friendship; for it passes away like a Flash of Lightning.

3. From a Woman's Love; for it changes upon every frivolous Fancy.

4. From Beauty; for the least Injury of Time, Misfortune, or a Disease destroys it.

5. From false Prayers; for they are but Smoak.

6. And from the Enjoyments of the World; for they all vanish in a Moment.

Men of Judgment, replied the Rat, are all of this Opinion; they never labour after these vain things; there is nothing but the Acquisition of a real Friend can tempt us to the Expectation of a lasting Happiness. The Raven then spoke in his turn. There is no earthly Pleasure or Advantage, said he, like a true Friend; which I shall endeavour to prove, by the Recital of the following Story.

F A B L E VIII.

A CERTAIN Person, of a truly noble and generous Disposition, once heard, as he lay in Bed, some body knocking at his Door at an unseasonable Hour. Something surprised at it, he, without stirring out of his Place, first ask'd, Who was there? But when by the Answer he understood that it was one of his best Friends, he immediately rose, put on his Cloaths, and ordering his Servant to light a Candle, went and opened the Door. So soon as he saw him, Dear Friend, said he, I at all time rejoice to see you, but doubly now, because I promise myself, from this extraordinery Visit, that I can be of some Service to you. I cannot imagine your coming so late to be for any other Reason, but either to borrow Money, to desire me to be your Second, or because you want Female Company to divert some sudden Melancholy: And I am very happy in that I can assure you that I am provided to serve you in any of these Requests. If you want Money, my Purse is full, and it is open to all your Occasions. If you are to meet with your Enemy, my Arm and Sword is at your Service. Or, if any amorous Desire brings you abroad, here is my Maid, handsome enough, and ready to give you a civil Entertainment. In a word, whatever lies in my Power is at your Service. There is nothing I have less Occasion for, answered his Friend, than all these things which you proffer me. I only came to understand the Condition of your Health, fearing the Truth of an unlucky and disastrous Dream.

While the Raven was reciting this Fable, our Set of Friends beheld at a distance a little wild Goat making towards them with an incredible Swiftness.

They all took it for granted, be her Speed, that she was pursued by some Hunter, and they immediately without Ceremony separated every one to take care of himself. The Tortoise slipt into the Water, the Rat crept into a Hole which he accidently found there, and the Raven hid himself among the Boughs of a very high Tree. In the mean time the Goat stopt all of a sudden, and stood to rest itself by the Side of the Fountain; when the Raven, who looked about every way, perceiving no body, called to the Tortoise, who immediately peeped up above the Water; and seeing the Goat afraid to drink, Drink bodly, said the Tortoise, for the Water is very clear: Which the Goat having done, Pray tell me, cried the Tortoise, what is the Reason you seem to be in such a Fright. Reason enough, replied the Goat, for I have just made my Escape from the Hands of a Hunter who pursued me with an eager Chase. Come, said the Tortoise, I am glad you are safe, and I have an Offer to make you, if you can like our Company, stay here, and be one of our Friends; you will find, I assure you, our Hearts honest and our Conversation beneficial. Wife Men, continued she, say, that the Number of Friends lessens Trouble; and that if a Man had a thousand Friends, he ought to reckon them no more than as one; but on the other Side, if a Man had but one Enemy, he ought to reckon that one for a thousand, so dangerous and so desperate a thing is an vowed Enemy. After this Discourse, the Raven and the Rat entered into Company with the Goat, and shewed her a thousand Civilities, with which she was so taken, that she promised to stay there as long as she lived.

These four Friends after this, lived in perfect good Harmony a long while, and spent their time very pleasantly together. But one Day as the Tortoise, the Rat, and the Raven, were met, as they used to do, by the Side of the

Fountain, the Goat was missing; this very much troubled the other Friends, as they knew not what Accident might have befallen her. They soon came to a Resolution, however, to seek for and assist her; and presently the Raven mounted up into the Air, to see what Discoveries he could make, and looked around about him, at length, to his great Sorrow, saw at a Distance the poor Goat entangled in a Hunter's Net. He immediately dropt down on this, to acquaint the Rat and Tortoise with what he had seen; and you may be well assured these ill Tidings extremely affficted all the three Friends. We have professed a strict Friendship together, and lived long happily in it, said the Tortoise, and it will be shameful now to break through it, and leave our innocent and good-natured Friend to destruction; no, we must find some Way, continued she, to deliver the poor Goat out of Captivity. On this said the Raven to the Rat, Remember now, Oh excellent *Zirac!* thy own Talents, and exert them for the public Good; there is none but you can set our Friend at liberty; and the Business must be quickly done, for fear the Huntsman lay his clutches upon her. Doubt not but I will gladly do my endeavour, replied the Rat; therefore let's go immediately, lest we lose time. The Raven on this took up *Zirac* in his Bill, and carried him to the Place; where being arrived, he fell without Delay to gnawing the Meashes that held the Goat's Foot, and had almost set him at liberty by the time the Tortoise arrived. So soon as the Goat perceived this slow-moving Friend, she sent forth a loud Cry: Oh! said she, why have you ventured yourself to come hither? Alas! replied the Tortoise, I could no longer endure your Absence. Dear Friend, said the Goat, your coming to this Place troubles me more than the Loss of my own Liberty: For if the Hunter should happen to come at this Instant, what will you do to make your Escape? For my part I am almost unbound, and my swift Heels will preserve me from falling into his hands; the Raven will find his Safety in his Wings; the Rat will run into any Hole; only you that are so slow of Foot will become the Hunter's Prey.

No sooner had the Goat spoken the Words but the Hunter appeared; but the Goat being unloosed ran away; the Raven mounted into the Sky, the Rat slip'd into a Hole, and, as the Goat had said, only the slow-paced Tortoise remained without Help.

When the Hunter arrived, he was not a little surprised to

see his Net broken. This was no small Vexation to him, and made him look narrowly about, to see if he could discover who had done him the Injury; and unfortunately in searching, he spied the Tortoise. On! said he, very well, I am very glad to see you here; I find I shan't go home empty-handed, however, at last: Here'a plump Tortoise, and that's worth something, I'm sure. With that he took the Tortoise up, put it in his Sack, threw the Sack over his Shoulder, and so was trudging home.

When he was gone, the three Friends came from their several Places, and met together, when missing the Tortoise, they easily judged what was become of her. Then sending forth a thousand Sighs, they made most doleful Lamentations, and shed a Torrent of Tears. At length, the Raven interrupting this sad Harmony, Dear Friends, said He, our Moans and Sorrows do the Tortoise no good; we ought, instead of this, if it be possible, to think of a Way to save her Life. The Sages of former Ages have informed us, that there are four Sorts of Persons that are never known but upon the proper Occasions; Men of Courage in Fight; Men of Honesty in Business; a Wife in her Husband's Misfortunes and a true Friend in extreme Necessity. We find, alas! our dear Friend the Tortoise is in a sad Condition, and therefore we must, if possible, succour her. 'Tis well advised, replied the Rat, and now I think on't an Expedient is come into my Head. Let the Goat go and shew herself in the Hunter's Eye, who will then be sure to lay down his Sack to run after her. Very well advised, replied the Goat, I will pretend to be lame, and run limping at a little Distance before him, which will encourage him to follow me, and so draw him a good Way from his Sack, which will give the Rat time to set our Friend at Liberty. This Stratagem had so good a Face, that it was soon approved by them all, and immediately the Goat ran halting before the Hunter, and seemed to be so feeble and faint, that the Hunter thought he had her safe in his Clutches; and so laying down his Sack, ran after the Goat with all his Might. That cunning Creature suffered him ever and anon almost to come up to her, and then led him another Green-goose Chase, till in short she had fairly dragged him out of Sight; which the Rat perceiving, came and gnawed the String that tied the Sack, and let out the Tortoise, who went and hid herself in a thick Bush.

At length the Hunter, tired with running in vain after his Prey, left off the Chace and returned to his Sack. Here, said he, I have something safe however, thou art not quite so swift of Foot as this plaguy Goat; and if thou wert, art too fast here to find the Way to make thy Legs of any Use to thee: So saying he went to the Bag, but there missing the Tortoise he was in Amaze, and thought himself in a Region of Hobgoblins and Spirits. He could not but stand and bless himself, that a Goat should free herself out of his Nets, and by and by run hopping before him, and make a Fool of him; and that in the mean while a Tortoise, a poor feeble Creature, should break the String of a Sack, and make its Escape. All these Considerations struck him with such a panic Fear, that he ran home as if a thousand Robin-goodfellows or Raw-head-and-Bloody-bones had been at his Heels. After which the four Friends met together again, congratulated each other on their Escapes, and made new Protestations of Friendship, and swore never to separate till Death parted them.

C H A P. V.

That we ought always to distrust our E N E M I E S, *and be, if possible, perfectly informed of whatever passes among them.*

WE are now, said *Dabschelim*, most exlent Man! come to the fifth Chapter, which is to prove, that no Person of Judgment and Discretion ought to hope for Friendship from his Enemies. Teach me therefore, most venerable Sage, since I must never expect good Offices from them, which Way to avoid their Treasons. We ought, replied the *Bramin*, always to distrust our Enemies; when they make a Shew of Friendship, 'tis only to cover their evil Designs. Whoever confides in the Enemy, believe me, will be deceived, like the Owl in the Fable which I am going to recite to your Majesty.

FABLE I.

The RAVENS *and the* OWLS.

In the north-west Parts of *Zamardot*,* continued *Pilpay*, there is a Mountain whose Top reaches above the Clouds; and near the Top of this Mountain there once stood a Tree whose Boughs seemed to reach Heaven: and these Boughs were all laden with the Nests of a vast Number of Ravens, who were all the Subject of a King called *Birouz*. One Night, the King of the Owls, who was called *Chabahang*, that is to say, *Fly by Night*, came at the Head of his Army (for the Birds of that Nation are all under the Government of their particular Monarchs) to plunder the Ravens Nests, against whom he had an ancient Hatred. That Night however they could do no more than make Preparations for their intended Enterprize, and by the vile Noise of their Screams defy the Enemy. The next Day *Birouz* called a Council, to deliberate what Means they should make use of to defend themselves from the Assaults of the Owls. On which five of the ablest Politicians of his Court understanding his

---

* *Zamardot* is accounted the most mountainous Country of all the East.

Majesty's Intentions, gave their Advice one after another in the following Words. Great Monarch, said the first, we can think of nothing but what your Majesty had unquestionably already thought of before us. Nevertheless, since 'tis your Pleasure that we should speak in order what we judge most expedient to revenge ourselves upon the Owls, I shall only presume to observe to your Majesty, that our best Politicians have always held for a Maxim, that no Prince ought ever to attack an Enemy stronger than himself: T o do otherwise, is to bbild upon the Current of a swift River. Sir, said the second, All I have to say is, that Flight becomes none but mean and cowardly Souls: 'Tis more noble to take Arms and revenge the Affront we have received, than tamely to bear it, were we sure it would be no worse. A Prince can never be at rest, if he does not carry Terror into the Country and into the Soul of his Enemy. When he had done speaking, the third coming to give his Opinion, said, I do not blame the Counsel of my Brethren who have already spoken; nor do I think either, or what may be deduced from both, sufficient. If I may presume to speak freely, my Advice is, that your Majesty send Spies, to discover the Strength and Condition of the Enemy; and according to the Tenor of their Reports, let us make War or Peace. It is the Duty of a King to preserve Peace in his own Kingdom, if it may be done without great Disadvantages, as well for the Repose of his own Mind as for the Ease of his Subjects. War, we all know, is never to be declared but against those that disturb the public Tranquility; and even in regard to such, if the Enemy be too powerful, we must have Recourse to Artifice and Stratagem, and make use of all Opportunities that present themselves, to vanquish him by Cunning and Policy. When this Politician had this given in his Opinion, the fourth took his Turn, and laid before the King, that, in his Opinion, it was better for a Prince even to quit his Country, than to expose a People to lose the Reputation of their Arms, who had always been victorious over their Enemies. That even though it should be found that the Enemies were the stronger, it would yet be a Shame for the Ravens to submit themselves to the Owls, who had all along been under their Subjection. And finally, that it was requisite to penetrate their Designs, and resolve rather to fight, than undergo an ignominions Yoke, since Loss of Life was less to be dreaded than Loss of Reputation.

The King, after he had heard these four Ministers, made a Signal to the fifth to speak in his Turn. The Vizier, or Minister, was called *Carchenas*, or the *Intelligent*. And the King, who had a particular Confidence in him, desired him to tell him sincerely what he though was best to be done in this Affair. What say you, *Carchenas?* said the Monarch, What shall we do? Shall we declare War, or propound Peace, or adandon our Country? Sir, replied *Carchenas*, since you order me to speak with Freedom, my Opinion is, that we ought not to attack the Owls, for this plain Reason, that they are more numerous than we. We must make use of Prudence, a Virtue that has frequently a greater Share in Successes than either Strength or Riches. But before your Majesty take your final Resolution, let me advise, that you consult your Ministers once more, and give them an Opportunity of declaring their Opinions a second Time; now that they are each of them acquainted with what is to be said on the other Side, their Councils may assist you to bring about your Designs with Success. Great Rivers are always swelled by many Rivulets. And for my part, I neither love War, nor am I for base and dastardly Submission. 'Tis not for Men of Honour to desire that they may have long Life, but that they may leave to Posterity Examples of Virtue worthy of Admiration: Nor ought we meanly to take care of our Lives at the Expense of our Country's Safety, but to expose them upon all Occasions where Honour calls us, considering 'tis better never to have been, than to live ignobly. Permit me to add, that my final Advice is, that your Majesty shew not the least Fear in this Conjuncture; and that you take your Resolutions in private, that your Enemies may not penetrate into your Designs.

Here one of the other Ministers interrupting *Carchenas*, said with some Earnestness, How! what mean you by this Advice, so different from the Tenor of the Beginning of your Speech. Wherefore are Councils held but to debate among several? And wherefore would you have an Affair of this Consequence decided in a private Manner? Affairs of Princes, replied *Carchenas*, are not like those on Merchants, which are to be communicated to the whole Society: And there is Difference between hearing the Advice of others and communicating our Designs to them. The Secrets of Kings cannot be discovered but by their Counsellors and Embassadors. And who knows but there may be Spies in this very Place who hear us, with an intent to disclose our Resolutions to our Enemies, who upon their Report will prevent our Enterprizes, or at least disorder our Determinations? Wise Men say, that if you will have a Secret, take care to keep it a Secret from all the World, not only from Enemies but from Friends. And let me tell you, Sir, that Monarch who does not observe this Rule, will run the Hazard of being betrayed, as was the King of *Quechemir*. Upon this *Birouz*, who was very curious, commanded *Carchenas* to tell him the History.

F A B L E II.

The KING *and his* MISTRESS.

IN the City of *Quechemir* there once reigned a King no less just than powerful, who had a Mistress so surpassingly beautiful, that all Persons that beheld her were in love with her. The King himself doated on her to that Degree, that he would never be out of her Company: But such was the Misfortune of their Destiny, that she was far from loving the King so dearly as she was beloved by him. The Affection of the King, in short, flattered her Vanity, but never touched her Heart; which being always made, however, to habour some particular Amour or other, she once suffered herself to be possessed with a violent Passion for a Page, who was handsome and well-proportioned, even to Admiration. She soon informed him by her Glances what Sentiments she had for him, and the ogling Youth as soon instructed her that she could not apply herself to a young Spark that was more inclined to make his Advantage of so fair a Fortune. In short, there wanted nothing but an Opportunity to get together in private.

In the midst of this Expectation of Happiness, it happened, however, that one Day as the King was sitting with his Mistress, and gazing on her with Delight, the Page who was standing in the same Chamber, cast his Eyes from time to time upon the charming Lady; while she, on the other hand, fixed hers upon the Page, with an Air so passionate, that the King plainly perceived it. He understood but too well that silent Language, and was so enraged with Jealousy and Distration, that he immediately resolved to put them both to Death. However, dissembling his Design, because he would not act with too much Precipitation, he re-entered his Apartment, where he spent the Night in miserable Uneasiness and Disquiet. The next Morning as soon as he arose, he heard the Complaints of his Subjects, as was his usual Custom; and after he had given Satisfaction to his People, entered into his Cabinet in great Disorder of Mind, and thither sent for his chief Minister, and disovered to him his Design to poison both his Mistress and the Page. The Vizier having heard his Reasons, told him, that he could not but approve them, and promised to keep the Secret. From his Master's Closet he immediately went home; where finding his Daughter extremely pensive, he asked the Reason, Father, said she, the King's favourite Mistress had publicly affronted me: I am distracted at it; and if I do not revenge myself, it is not for want of good Will. Comfort yourself, replied the Minister, take my Word for it, you will soon be delivered from your Pain.

Now as the Women are naturally very curious, the Daughter, from this Hint, continually pressed her Father to know after what manner she should be revenged on her Enemy; and he was at length so weak as to reveal to her the King's Design. It is true, she swore not to discover it. But an Hour or two after, the King's Mistress's Eunuch coming to visit the Minister's Daughter, with an Intention to comfort her, and extenuate the Affront she had received; and to that Purpose telling her, that we ought to bear with our Neighbour's Faults: Ay, ay, said the lady, interrupting him, with a disdainful Smile, let her alone, she has not long to play her proud Pranks. Upon which the Eunuch pressed her so earnestly to explain her Meaning, that she could hold no longer, but told him every Word that her Father had said to her, after she had made him also swear, that he would inviolably keep the Secret. The Eunuch, however, did not think an Oath of that kind very binding; and, in short, he no sooner left her, but believing himself much more obliged to break than to keep his Protestations of Secrecy, he went to the King's Mistress, and revealed to her the violent Resolution which the King had taken. There needed no more than the Knowledge of the Intent of the King, you may be sure, to incense the Lady to try all ways to prevent and to be revenged on him. In short, she sent away privately for the Page, with whom she took such Measures, that the King was found next Morning dead in his Bed.

You see by this Story, continued *Carchenas,* that Princes are not to discover their Secrets to any, at least not to any but those of whose Discretion and Fidelity they have had constant and assured Proofs. But of what Nature are the Secrets, said *Birouz,* which it most of all concerns us to conceal? Sir, answered *Carchenas,* there are many Kinds of Secrets: Some are of such a Nature that Princes are not to entrust any body but themselves with them; that is to say, they ought to keep them so concealed that nobody may be able from any thing they see, even to make the least Guess at them: And others there are, which tho' they ought to be kept most sacredly from the general Knowledge, yet they may be communicated to faithful Ministers for their Advice and Counsel.

Birouz finding that *Carchenas* spoke nothing but Reason, withdrew from the rest of the Council, and shut himself up with him in his Cabinet; and before he discoursed at large concerning the Business in question, he desired him to tell him the fatal Original of the deadly and hereditary Hatred between the Ravens and the Owls. Sir, answered *Carchenas,* a few Words alone produced that cruel Animosity, the terrible Effects of which you have so oft experienced. The Story at large is this:

F A B L E III.

The Original of the Hatred between the RAVENS *and the* OWLS.

IT once happened that in the Neighbourhood of this our delightful Habitation, a Flight of Birds assembled to chuse themselves a King; and every different Species among them put in his Pretensions to the Crown. At length, however, there were several that gave their Voices for the Owl, because *Minerva* the Goddess of Wisdom, had made choice of the Owl for her perculiar Bird; But a vast Number of others being strenuous in their Resolution never to obey so deformed a Creature, the Diet broke up, and they fell one upon another with so much Fury, that several on all Sides were slain. The Fight, however, probably would have lasted longer than it did, had not a certain Bird, in order to part them, bethought himself of crying out to the Combatants, No more civil Wars; why do you spill one another's Blood in vain, here is a Raven coming, let us all agree to make him our Judge and Arbitrator; he is a Person of Judgment, and whose Years have gained him Experience. The Birds unanimously consented to this; and when the Raven arrived, and had informed himself of the Occasion of the Quarrel, he thus delivered himself: Are you such Fools and

Madmen, Gentlemen, says he to chuse for your King a Bird, that draws after him nothing but Misfortune? Will you set up a Fly instead of a Griffin? Why do you not rather make choice of a Falcon, who is eminent for his Courage and Agility? or else a Peacock, who treads with a majestic Gait, and carries a Train of starry Eyes in his Tail? Why do you not rather raise an Eagle to the Throne, who is the Emblem of Royalty; or, lastly, a Griffin, who only by the Motion and Noise of his Wings makes the Mountains tremble? But tho' there were no such Birds as these that I have named in the World, surely it were better for you to live without a King, than subject yourselves to such a horrid Creature as an Owl; for tho' he has the Physyognomy of a Cat he has no Wit; and which is yet more insupportable, notwithstanding that is so abominably ugly, he is as proud as a fine Lady at a public Feast: And which ought, if possible, to render him yet more despicable in our Eyes, he hates the Light of that magnificent Body that enlivens all Nature. Therefore, Gentlemen, lay aside a Design so prejudicial to your Honour, proceed to the Election of another King, and do nothing that you may be sure to repent of afterwards. Chuse a King that may comfort you in your Distresses, and remember the Story of the Rabbet who calling himself the Moon's Embassador, expelled the Elephants out of his Country.

F A B L E IV.

The ELEPHANTS *and the* RABBETS.

THERE happened once, continued the Raven, a most dreadful Year of Drought in the Elephants Country, called the *Isles of Rad,* or of the *Wind,* insomuch that, pressed by extreme Thirst, and not being able to come at any Water, the whole Body of the Nation at length publicly addressed themselves to their King, beseeching him to apply some Remedy to their Misery, that they might not perish, or to destroy them all at once, rather than let them endure Life of so much Misery. The King, upon this passionate Application, commanded diligent Search to be made in all Places in the Neighbourhood, or at any reasonable Distance: And at length there was discovered a Spring of Water; to which the Ancients had given the Name of *Chaschmanah,* or the *Fountain of the Moon.* Immediately on this most happy Discovery, the King came and encamped with his whole Army in the Parts adjoining this Fountain: But, as Misfortune would have it, the coming of the Elephants ruined a great Number of Rabbets that had a Warren in the same Place, because the Elephants, every Step they took, trod down their Burroughs, and killed the poor Creatures Young-ones.

The Rabbets, on this public Calamity, assembled together, went to their King, and besought him to deliver them from this terrible Oppression. I know very well, answered the King, that I sit upon the Throne only for the Welfare and Ease of my Subjects; but alas! you now ask me a Thing that far surpasses my Strength. Upon this one Rabbet, more cunning than the rest, perceiving the King at a loss, yet very much moved with the Affliction of his People, stept before his Companions, and addressing himself to the King, Sir, said he, your Majesty thinks like a just and generous Prince; while the Care of our Tranquility disturbs your Rest, and while you afford us the Freedom to give our Advice, it makes me bold to impart to your Majesty an Invention lately come into my Head, to drive those terrible Destroyers, the Elephants, out of this Country. Permit me only, continued the Rabbet, that I may go with the Character of your Embassador to the King of the Elephants, and doubt not but I will send all these Strangers away faster than they came; neither need your Majesty to fear that I shall make any improper Submissions to them; if any Thought of that kind in the least disturbs your Majesty's Breast, I am willing that your Majesty should appoint me a Companion, who may, at any time, return to you, and acquaint you with all that passes in my Embassy

No, replied the King very obligingly, go alone and prosper; I will have no Spies upon thy Actions; for I believe thee faithful; go, in the Name of Heaven, and do what thou shalt deem most convenient, only take care that you always remember that an Embassador is the King's Tongue; his Discourses therefore ought to be well weighed, and his Words and his Behaviour noble, and such as would suit the Prince himself, whom he represents. The most learned in the Kingdom ought always to be made choice of for Embassadors. Nay, I have heard that one of the greatest Monarchs in the World was wont frequently to disguise himself, and become his own Embassador. Indeed, for the honourable and proper Discharge of that Employment, three neccessary Qualities are Resolution, Eloquence, and a vast Extent of natural Parts. A violent Spirit, let me tell you, is not for that Employment. Several Embassadors, with a rash Word, have created Trouble in a peaceful Kingdom: And others, with a mild and agreeable Saying, have re-united irreconcileable Enemies. Sir, said the Rabbet, if I am not endowed with these good Qualities your Majesty has enumerated, I will endeavour, at least, to make the best of those I have; and shall ever remember this Lesson, which your Majesty has honoured me with, and endeavour to act according to what your Majesty has so justly declared to be the Duty of one in so public and so honourable an Employment.

Having so said, he took leave of the King, and went immediately forward on his Journey to the Elephants. Before he ventured himself among them, however, he bethought himself, that if he went into the Croud that usually attended on that King, he might very likely be trod to Pieces: For which Reason he got upon a high Tree, from whence he called to the King of the Elephants, who was not far off, and addressed himself in the following Words: I am, said he, the Moon's Embassador, hear therefore with Reverence and Attention what I have to say to you in her Name. You, who in Ages have been famous for your Adorations of my Royal Mistress, know full well, I doubt not, that the Moon is a Goddess whose Power is unlimited, and that above all things she hates a Lye.

The King of the Elephants, who was a just and most pious Prince, trembled when he heard the Rabbet talk of these things, and humbly desired to know the Subject of his Embassy. The Moon, replied the Rabbet, has sent me hither, to let you understand, that whoever is puffed up with his own Grandeur, and despises her little ones, deserves Death, and that she is grieved to see that you are not contented only to oppress the little ones, our peaceful and religious Nation, but you have the Insolence to trouble a Fountain consecrated to her Deity, where every thing is pure. Reform your Manners, else you will be severely punished. And if you will not give Credit to my Words, come and see the Moon in her own Fountain, and then tremble and retire.

The King of the Elephants was inwardly grieved and astonished at these Words, and went to the Fountain, wherein he saw the Moon indeed, because the Water was so clear, and the Moon then shone very brightly. Then said the Rabbet to the Elephant, You see the sacred Deity; take of the Water to wash yourself, and pay your Adorations. The Elephant very obediently took some of the Water, but puddled the Fountain with his Trunk: At which the Rabbet,

Infidel, said he, you have prophaned the Fountain with your unhallowed Touch, and behold, the Goddess is gone away in a Passion, retire, therefore, I conjure you with Speed from hence with your whole Army, lest some dreadful Misfortune befal you. This threatning Language put the King of the Elephants into a trembling, and terrified him to that Degree, that he presently commanded his Army to decamp; and away they all marched, never to return to the sacred Fountain of the Moon again. And thus the Rabbets were delivered from their Enemies by the Policy of one of their Society.

I have not recited this Example, continued the Raven, but to instruct you, that you ought to make choice of a prudent and politic Bird for your Sovereign, since by it you see, that Art and Address, even in the Representative of a King only, can do more than Force in many Cases, tho' the King himself and his whole Army engaged in the Enterprize. Chuse therefore one for your King who may be able to assist you in your Adversities, and not an Owl, who has neither Courage nor Wit. These obscene Birds have nothing in them but Malice, which will, one time or other, believe me, be no less fatal to you than the Cat once was to the Partridge, who desired him to decide a Difference which she had with another Bird. The Story is this:

FABLE V.

The CAT *and the* TWO BIRDS.

SOME Years ago, continued the Raven, I made my Nest upon a Tree, at the Foot of which there frequently sat a Partridge, a fair and comely Bird, well shaped and good-humoured: Our neighbouring Situation soon brought us acquainted with one another; and after a short Knowledge of each other's Talents and Humour, we made a League of Friendship together, and almost continually kept one another Company. Some time after our first entering on this Intimacy one with another, my Friend, however, absented herself, for what Reason I know not, and staid away so long, that I thought her dead: but my Thoughts of this kind were mistaken, for she at length returned, but had the Misfortune to find her Habitation in Possession of another Bird. The Partridge pretended the House was hers, and would have made a forcible Entry: but the Bird refused to go out, alledging that Possession was the strongest Tenure of the Law. I endeavoured, soon after this, to bring them to an Accommodation, but all to no Purpose; for the Partridge's Attorney finding she had Money, egged her on, and tickled her Ears with a Leafe of Ejectment.

However, at length, the Partridge, finding the Law to be very tedious and very expensive, said one Day to herself, here lives hard by, I remember, a very devout Cat, she fasts every Day, does no body Harm, and spends the Nights in Prayer: Let us, in short, said she to her Adversary, distract our Brains and empty our Purses no more about Law, but refer our Difference to her: I know not where we shall find a more equitable Judge. The other Bird having consented to this Proposal, they went both to this religious Cat, and I followed them out of Curiosity. Entering, I saw the Cat very attentive at a long Prayer, without turning either to the Right or Left, which put me in mind of the old Proverb, that *long Prayers before People is the Key of Hell*. I admired the sober Hypocrisy, and had the Patience to stay till the venerable Personage had done. After which the Partridge and his Antagonist accosted him with great Respect, and requested him to hear their Difference, and give Judgment according to the usual Rules of Justice. The Cat in his Fur Gown acting the Part of a grave and formal Judge, first heard what the Stranger-bird had to plead for itself, and then addressing himself to the Partridge, My pretty Love, said he, come you now to me and let me hear your Story; but as I am old and thick of hearing, pray come near and lift up your Voice, that I may not lose a Word of what you say. The Partridge and the other Bird on this, seeing him so devout and sanctified, both went boldly close up to him; but then the Hypocrite discovered the Bottom of his Sanctity, for he immediately fell upon them, and in short devoured them both.

You see by this Example, continued he, that deceitful People are never to be trusted: And my Inference from all this is, Have you a care of the Owl, who is the truth no better than the Cat. The Birds convinced that the Raven spoke nothing but what was Reason, never minded the Owl any more; and upon this the Owl went home, meditating how to be revenged upon the Raven, against whom he conceived such a mortal Hatred, that Time could never extinguish it.

This, Sir, proceeded *Carchenas*, is the true Reason of the perpetual Enmity between us and the Owls. I thank you, Vizier, for this Story, replied the Monarch; and now let us consider what Measures we must take to preserve the Peace of my Subjects, and revenge the Affront I have received. To which *Carchenas*, making a low Reverence, replied, Sir, Permit me to speak my Mind freely, and inform your

Majesty, that I am not of the same Opinion with your other Ministers, who advise either War, or Flight, or an ignominious Peace. I dissent from all, and would only recommend to your Majesty to take at present no absolute Resolution at all, but to follow cautiously this excellent Maxim, that when we want Strength, we must have Recourse to Artifice and Stratagem, and endeavour to deceive the Enemy, by feigning one thing and doing another. The Advantage of this way of proceeding in Things of this kind, we may see by the following Example.

F A B L E VI.

The DERVISE *and the* FOUR ROBBERS.

A DERVISE had once made a Purchase of a fine fat Sheep, with intent to offer it up in Sacrifice; and having tied a Cord about the Neck of it, was leading it to his Habitation: But as he led it along, four Thieves perceived him, and had a great mind to steal his Sacrifice for less holy Uses. They dared not, however, take it away from the Dervise by Force, because they were too near the City, therefore they made use of this Stratagem; they first parted Company, and then accosted the Dervise, whom they knew to be an honest and inoffensive Man, and one who thought of no more Harm in others than he had in himself, as if they had come from several distinct Parts. Said the first of them, who had contrived to meet him full face, Father, whither are you leading this Dog? At this Instant the second coming from another Quarter, cried to him, Venerable old Gentleman, I hope you have not so far forgot yourself as to have stolen this Dog. And immediately after him the third coming up and asking him, Whether he would go a coursing with that handsome Grey-hound? The poor Dervise began to doubt whether the Sheep which he had was a Sheep or no. But the fourth Robber put him quite beside himself, coming up at that Instant, and saying to him, Pray, Reverend Father, what did this Dog cost you? The Dervise on this, absolutely persuaded that four Men, coming from four several Places, could not all be deceived, verily believed that the Grasier who had sold him the Sheep was a Conjuror, and had bewitched his Sight; insomuch that no longer giving Credit to his own Eyes, he began to be firmly convinced that the Sheep he was leading was a Dog; and immediately in full Persuasion of it, went back to Market to demand his Money of the Grasier, leaving the Weather with the Felons, who carried it away.

Sir, said *Carchenas*, your Majesty sees by this Example, that what cannot be done by Force, must be atchieved by Policy. You advise me well, said the King; and now tell me by what Invention shall we revenge ourselves on the Owls? Rely upon me, replied *Carchenas*, to take care of your Majesty's Revenge, and suffer me to sacrifice my own private Ease to the public Good. Only order my Feathers to be pulled off, and leave all over bloody under this Tree, and doubt not but I will do you an acceptable Service. 'Twas no small Grief to *Birouz* to give out such a cruel Order. In regard to this excellent Minister, however, at his own incessant Intreaties, the Thing at length was done, and the King marched away with his Army to wait for *Carchenas* in a Place where that Vizier had appointed him.

In the mean time Night came, and the Owls, puffed up with the Success of the Insolence the Night before, returned, intending now, by a bloody Battle, at once to complete the Destruction of the Ravens. But they were amazed when they missed the Enemy, whom they intended to have surprized. They sought for the Ravens Army diligently from every Corner, and in their Searches they heard a Voice of grievous Lamentation, which was the Voice of *Carchenas* who was lamenting at the Foot of a Tree. The King of the Owls on this immediately approached him, and examined him concerning his Birth, and the Employment he had in *Birouz's* Court? Alas! replied *Carchenas*, the Condition wherein you see me sufficiently shews you my Inability to give you the Account which you demand. I have not Strength, alas! to repeat it. What Crime did you commit then, replied *Chabahang*, to deserve this hard Usage? No

Crime, O mighty Monarch! replied *Carchenas*; but the wicked Ravens, upon a slight Suspicion only, have used me thus. After our Army, continued he, was thrown into Terror and Affright last Night by your bold Defiance, King *Birouz* called a Council, to seek out Ways to be revenged of so hainous an Affront. And after he had heard the various Opinions of some of his Ministers, he commanded me to speak mine: At which Time I laid before him, that you were not only superior in Number, but better disciplined, and more valiant than we were; and by consequence that it was necessary for us to desire Peace, and to accept of whatever Conditions you would be pleased to grant us. This so incensed the King against me, that in a violent Passion, Traitor, cried he, this is the Way to infuse into my Army a Fear of the Enemy, by exalting their Strength and lessening mine; and with that, suspecting that I was meditating to seek my Peace with your Majesty, he commanded that I should be used as you see.

After *Carchenas* had done speaking, the King of the Owls asked his chief Minister what was to be done with him? The only Way, Sir, answered the Minister, is to put him out of his Pain, and knock him o' the Head; never trust his fair Speeches, for I don't believe a Word he says. Remember the old Proverb, Sir, *The more dead, the fewer Enemies.* *Carchenas* on this, in a lamentable Tone, cried out, I beseech you, Sir, add not to my Affliction by your threatning Language.

The King of the Owls, who could not chuse but compassionate *Carchenas*, now bid the second Minister speak; who was not of the first Vizier's Opinion. Sir, said he, I would not advise your Majesty to put this Person to Death. Kings ought to assist the Weak, and succour those that throw themselves into their Protection. Besides, continued he, sometimes there may be great Advantage made of an Enemy's Service, according to the Story of a certain Merchant, which, with Permission, I will relate to your Majesty.

FABLE VII.

The MERCHANT, *his* WIFE, *and the* ROBBER.

THERE was once, continued the Minister, a certain Merchant, very rich, but homely, and very deformed in his Person, who had married a very fair and virtuous Wife. He loved her passionately; but, on the other hand, she hated him, insomuch, that not being able to endure him, she lay herself in a separate Bed in the same Chamber.

It happened, soon after they were married, that a Thief one Night broke into the House, and came into the Chamber. The Husband was at this Time asleep; but the Wife being awake, and perceiving the Thief, was in such a terrible Fright, that she ran to her Husband, and caught him fast in her Arms. The Husband waking, was transported with Joy to see the Delight of this Life clasping him in her Embraces. Bless me! cried he, to what am I obliged for this extraordinary Happiness? I wish I knew the Person to whom I owe it, that I might return him thanks. Hardly had he uttered the Words when the Thief appeared, and he soon guessed the whole Occasion. Oh! cried the Merchant, the most welcome Person in the World; take whatever thou thinkest fitting, I cannot reward thee sufficiently for the good Service thou hast done me.

By this Example we may see that our Enemies may sometimes be serviceable to us, in obtaining those Things which we have sought in vain to enjoy by the Help of our Friends. So that since this Raven may prove beneficial to us, we ought, I am of Opinion, to preserve his Life.

The King, on this Minister's ending his Speech, asked a third what he thought; who delivered his Opinion in these Words. Sir, said he, so far from putting this Raven to Death, you ought to caress him, and engage him by your Favours to do you some important Service. The Wife always endeavour to oblige some of their Enemies, in order to set up a Faction against the rest, and then make advantage of their Divisions. The Quarrel which the Devil once had with the Thief, was the Reason that neither the one nor the other could hurt a very virtuous Dervise, according to the ensuing Fable.

F A B L E VIII.

The DERVISE, *the* THIEF, *and the* DEVIL.

IN the Parts adjoining to *Babylon*, continued the third Minister, there was once a certain Dervise who lived like a true Servant of Heaven: He subsisted only upon such Alms as he received; and as for other things gave himself up wholly to Providence, without troubling his Mind with the Intrigues of this World.

One of the Friends of the Dervise, one Day sent him a fat Ox; which a Thief seeing as it was led to his Lodging, resolved to have it whatever it cost him: With this Intent he set forward for the Dervise's Habitation; but as he went on, he met the Devil in the Shape of a plain-dressed Man, and suspecting by his Countenance, that he was one of his own Stamp, he immediately asked him who he was, and whither he was going? The Stranger on this, made him a short Answer to his Demand; saying I am the Devil, who have taken human Shape upon me, and I am going to this Cave, with intent to kill the Dervise that lives there; because his Example does me a world of Mischief, by making several wicked People turn honest and good Men: I intend therefore to put him out of the Way, and then hope to succeed better in my Business than I have done of late, else I assure you we shall soon want People in my Dominions. Mr. Satan, answered the Thief, I am your most obedient humble Servant; I assure you I am one you have no Reason to complain about, for I am a notorious Robber, and am going to the same Place whither you are bent, to steal a fat Ox that was, a few Hours ago, given to the Dervise that you design to kill. My good Friend, quoth the Devil, I am heartily glad I have met you, and rejoice that we are both of the same Honour, and that both of us design to do this abominable Dervise a Mischief. Go on and prosper, continued the Devil, and know when you rob such People as these, you do me a doubly acceptable Service.

In the midst of this Discourse they came both to the Dervise's Habitation; Night was already well advanced; and the good Man had said his usual Prayers, and was gone to bed. And now the Thief and the Devil were both preparing to put their Designs in Execution; when the Thief said to himself, the Devil in going to kill this Man will certainly make him cry out, and raise the Neighbourhood, which will hinder me from stealing the Ox. The Devil, on the other hand, reasoned with himself after this Manner: If the Thief goes to steal the Ox, before I have executed my Design, the Noise he will make in breaking open the Door will waken the Dervise, and set him on his Guard. Therefore said the Devil to the Thief, let me first kill the Dervise, and then thou mayest steal the Ox at thy own leisure; no, said the Thief, the better Way will be for you to stay till I have stolen the Ox, and then do you murder the Man. But both refusing to give way the one to the other, they quarrelled first, and from Words they fell to downright Fisty-Cuffs. At which Sport the Devil proving the stronger of the two, the Thief called out to the Dervise, Awake Man, arise, here is the Devil come to murder you. And on this the Devil perceiving himself discovered, cried out, Thieves, Thieves, look to your Ox, Dervise. The good Man quickly waking at the Noise, called in the Neighbours, whose Presence constrained the Thief and the Devil to betake themselves to their Heels: And the poor Dervise saved both his Life and his Ox.

The chief Minister having heard this Fable, falling into a very great Passion, said to the King, Listen, not, O sacred Sir, I beseech you, to these idle Stories: If you give way to what they would insinuate, believe me, you will suffer yourself to be decived by this Raven, not less than the Joiner was deceived by his Wife. What is that Story, replied *Chabahang?* go on and relate it to me.

F A B L E IX.

The JOINER *and his* WIFE.

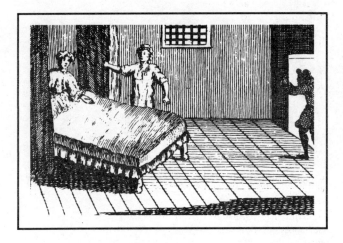

IN the City of *Guaschalla*, Sir, continued the Minister then,
there once lived a Joiner, who was very skillful in his Art,
and the Husband of a Wife so beautiful that the Sun seemed
to borrow his Brightness from her Eyes; and she was so
passionately beloved by her Husband, that he was almost
out of his Wits when he was constrained to be absent but for
a Moment from her. This fine Lady on her part was so
crafty, that she had found the Way to make her Husband
believe she loved him as dearly as he did her; and had no
Pleasure but in his Company, though at the same time she
had several Gallants that were not unacceptable to her.
Among the rest there was a Neighbour of hers, a young
Man well shaped, and with a good Face, who had won her
Affection to that Degree, that she began to care for none of
the rest. Upon which they became so jealous of him, that,
despairing of any good Luck for themselves, in revenge,
they gave the Joiner notice of his Familiarity with his Wife.
The honest Husband, however, was unwilling to believe any
thing, unless he were well assured; and therefore, that he
might be certain of a Truth which he was yet afraid to know,

he pretended one Day that he was to go a small Journey; and taking some Provisions with him, told his Wife that it was true he should not go very far, but his Business he was afraid would keep him out two or three Days; and that it would be a great Trouble to him to want her Company so long; but that he must endeavour to support himself under it with the Thoughts of her Goodness. His Wife paid him in the same Coin, bemoaning the Tediousness of his Absence, and shedding an *April* Shower of Tears rather for Joy than Grief. The Lady soon got every thing ready for her Husband's Departure; and he, the better to dissemble the Matter, bid her to be sure to keep the Doors fast for fear of Thieves. She, on the other Side, promised to be very careful of every thing, and still put on a Shew of the deepest Melancholy, for grief that he was to leave her. Her Husband's Back was no sooner turned, however, but she gave notice to her Gallant to come to her, who kept his time to a Minute. In short, he was there before the Joiner was well gone, and a World of Happiness they were fondly promising themselves. But while they were dallying together, the Joiner returned home, entered without being seen, and clapt himself into a Corner to see how Things went.

The Gallant now every Moment most eagerly caressed his Mistress, who admitted his Fondnesses with Delight. In fine, they supped together, and then made themselves ready to go to Bed.

The Joiner, who till then had seen nothing that could perfectly convince him if his Shame, stole softly toward the Bed, intending to take them in the Act; but the Wife having now luckily observed him, whispered her Lover in the Ear that he should ask her which she loved best, him or her Husband. Presently her Gallant, with a loud Voice, Don't you love me, my Dear, cried he, much better than your Husband? Why do you ask me so foolish a Question, answered the Wife? Know you not that Women, when they seem to shew any Friendship to any other Man but their Husbands, only do it to satisfy their Pleasure; and when they are satisfied, never think of their pretended Lover more? For my part, I assure you I idolize my Husband, I wear him always in my Heart; and in my Opinion, indeed, that Woman is unworthy to live, that loves not her Husband better than herself.

These Words were some kind of Cordial to the Joiner's Spirit, who began now to blame himself for the bad Opinion he had just before entertained of his Wife; saying to himself, the Fault which she now commits must be imputed to my Absence and the Frailty of her Sex. The chastest Person in the World sins either in Deed or Intention; and therefore since she loves me so well, I cannot but pardon her Offence, nor will I be so cruel to deprive her for a Moment of her Pleasure. After he had made these Reflexions, the courteous Spouse retired to his Corner, and let the two Lovers wanton together all the rest of the Night; which they did not without some Fear on the Lady's Side, who, when she saw no more of her Husband, thought her Eyes had deceived her, and ventured to Bed, but was not however without some Panics.

After a Night thus spent, the Lover early in the Morning arose and departed, and the Wife lay in Bed counterfeiting herself asleep. When the Husband, going to Bed in his Turn, fell to kissing and caressing her; and the Wife opening her Eyes, and dissembling astonishment, Laud! my dear Heart, said she to her Husband, how long have you been returned? Why I have been returned ever since last Night, replied the Joiner, but I was unwilling to disturb the young Man that lay with you, because I perceived that you had me in your Mind all the while you received his Caresses, which you would never have admitted but that you thought me absent. Upon these kind Words, the Wife frankly, and with a seeming Openness of Heart, confessed her Fault, and begged him never to be absent again.

This Example instructs us, Sir, that we are not to be lulled asleep with fair Words. Enemies, when they cannot obtain their Ends by Force, commonly have recourse to Artifices, and humble themselves to decieve us. Here *Carchenas* cried out, Oh! you that are so zealous for my Death, why do you not put an end at once to my Days, but talk so many things to no purpose to increase my Misery? What Probability is there of Perfidiousness in a Person so wounded as I am? What Madman would suffer so much Torment to do Good to another? It is in that very thing, replied the Vizier, that thy Subtilty consists. The Sweetness of Revenge which thou art meditating, makes thee patiently swallow the Bitterness of thy Pains. Thou wouldest sain make thyself as famous as the Monkey that sacrificed his Life to the Safety of his Country. I most humbly entreat the King to hear the Story.

F A B L E X.

The MONKEYS and the BEARS.

A Great Number of Monkeys once, continued he, lived in a Country well stored with all manner of Fruit, and very delightful. It happened one Day a Bear travelling that way by Accident, and considering the Beauty of the Residence, and the sweet Lives the Monkeys led, said to himself, it is not just nor reasonable that these little Animals should live so happy, while I am forced to run through Forests and Mountains in search of Food. Full of Indignation at this Difference of Fortune, he ran immediately among the Apes, and killed some of them for very Madness: But they all fell upon him; and in regard they were very numerous, they soon made him all over Wounds, so that he had much ado to make his Escape.

Thus punished for his Rashness, he made what haste he could to escape; and at length recovered a Mountain within hearing of some of his Comrades; and no sooner saw himself there, but he set up so loud a Roaring, that a great Number of Bears immediately came about him, to whom he recounted what had befallen him. When they had heard his Story out, instead of the Emotions he expected to have found in them, they all laughed at him: Thou are a most wretched Coward, cried they, to suffer thyself to be beaten by those little Animals. This is true, indeed, replied a leading Bear, but, however, this Affront is not to be endured; it must be revenged for the Honour of our Nation. On this they soon concerted proper Measures to annoy the Enemy; and toward the Beginning of the Night, decended all from the Mountain, and fell pell-mell upon the Monkeys, who were dreaming of nothing less than of such an Invasion; in short they were all retired to their Rest, when they were surrounded by the Bears, who killed a great Number, the rest escaping in Disorder. After this Exploit, the Bears were so taken with this Habitation, that they made choice of it for the Place of their own settled Abode. They set up for their King the Bear that had been so ill handled by the Monkeys; and after that fell to banquet upon the Provisions which the Monkeys had heaped together in their Magazines.

The next Morning by Break of the Day, the King of the Monkeys (who knew nothing of this fatal Calamity; for he had been hunting for two Days together) met several Monkeys maimed, who gave him an Account of what had passed the Day before. The King, when he heard this doleful News, immediately began to weep and lament the vast Treasure he had lost, accusing Heaven of Injustice, and Fortune of Inconstancy. In the midst of all his Indignation and Sorrow, his Subjects also pressed him to take his Revenge; so that the poor King knew not which way to turn himself. Now among the Monkeys that at that time attended on this Monarch, there was one called *Maimon*, who was one of the most crafty and most learned in the Court, and was the King's chief Favourite. This poor Creature, seeing his Master sad, and his Companions in Consternation, stood up and addressing himself to the King, Persons of Wit and Discretion, said he, never abandon themselves to Despair, which is a Tree that bears but very bad fruit; but Patience, on the contrary, supplies us with a thousand Inventions to rid ourselves out of this Intanglements of Trouble and Adversity.

The King, whom this Discourse had rendered much more easy in his Mind, turning to *Maimon,* on this said, But how shall we do, Vizier, to bring ourselves off with Honour from this ignominious Misfortune? *Maimon* besought his

Majesty, on this allow him private Audience; and after he had obtained it, he spoke to this effect.

Sir, said he, I conjure you by the dear Hopes of a great Revenge to hear me out with Patience. My Heart is as much distracted, O my sacred Master, for my private, if it be possible, as for the public Misfortune: My Wife and children have been massacred by these Tyrants. Imagine then my Grief, to see myself deprived for ever of those Sweets which I enjoyed in the Society of my Family: And hear me with Patience, and full Belief, when I assure you I am resolved to die, that I may put an end to my Sorrows: But my Death shall not be idle; no, I will find Means to make it prove fatal to my Royal Master's Enemies. O *Maimon*, said the King, consider we never desire to be revenged of our Enemies, but with Intent to procure to ourselves Repose or Satisfaction of Mind; but when you are dead, what signifies it to you, whether the World be at Wars or in Peace? Sir, replied *Maimon*, in the Condition I am in, Life being unsupportable to me, I sacrifice it with Delight to the Happiness of my Companions. All the Favour I beg of your Majesty, is only with Gratitude and Compassion to remember my Generosity when you shall be re-established in your Dominions. What I have farther to ask of you is this, that you will immediately command my Ears to be torn from my Head, my Teeth to be pulled out, and my Feet to be cut off; and then let me be left for the Night in a Corner of the Forest where we were lodged; then retire you, Sir, with the Remainder of your Subjects, and remove two Days Journey from hence, and on the third, you may return to your Palace; for you shall hear no more of your Enemies; and may you for ever reap the Blessings my Death intends you. The King, tho' with great Grief, caused *Maimon's* Desires to be executed, and left him in the Wood, where all Night he made the most doleful Lamentations that every Misery uttered.

When Day shone out, the King of the Bears, who had all Night long heard *Maimon's* Outcries, advanced to see what miserable Creature had made the Noise, and beholding the poor Monkey in that Condition, he was moved with Compassion, notwithstanding his merciless Humour, and asked him who he was, and who had used him after that barbarous Manner? *Maimon* judging, by all Appearances, that he was the King of the Bears that spoke to him, after he had respectfully saluted him, expressed himself in the following Words: Sir, said he, I am the King of the Monkeys chief Minister; I went, some Days ago, hunting with him and at our Return, understanding the Ravages which your Majesty's Soldiers had committed in Houses, he took me aside and asked me what was his best Course to take at such a Juncture? I answered him without any Hesitation, that we ought to put ourselves under your Protection, that we might live at Ease and unmolested. The King, my Master, then talked many ridiculous Things of your Majesty, which was the Reason that I took the Boldness to tell him, that you were a most renowned Prince, and beyond all Comparison more potent than he. Which Audaciousness of mine incensed him to that Degree, that immediately he commanded me to be thus mangled, as you see me.

Maimon had no sooner concluded his Relation, but he let fall such a Shower of Tears, that the King of Bears was molified also, and could not forbear weeping himself. When this was a little over, he asked *Maimon*, where the Monkeys were? In a Desart called *Mardazmay*, answered he, where they are raising a prodigious Army, the whole Place, for a thousand Leagues Extent, being inhabited by no other Creatures but Monkeys; and there is no question to be made made but they will be with you in a very short time. The King of the Bears, not a little terrified at this News, asked *Maimon*, whom he thought sufficiently exasperated against the Monkey Government to make his assured Friend, What Course he should take to secure himself from the Enterprises of the Monkeys? Face them boldly, replied *Maimon*, your Majesty need not fear them; were not my Legs broke, I would undertake with one single Troop of your Forces to destroy forty thousand of them. You advise me well, said the King, and, with your Help, I doubt not but I shall destroy them. There is no question but you know all the Avenues to their Camp. You will oblige us ever for ever, would you but conduct us thither; and be assured we will revenge the Barbarity committed upon your Person. That, alas! is impossible, replied *Maimon*, because I can neither go nor stand. There is a Remedy for every thing, answered the King, and I will find an Invention to carry you; and, at the same time, he gave Orders to his Army to be in readiness to march, and to put themselves into a Condition to fight. They all readily obeyed the Orders, and tied *Maimon*, who was to be their Guide, upon the Head of one of the biggest Bears.

Maimon now gloried in his Mind that he had it in his Power to revenge all that himself and his Country had suffered. And in order to it, conducted them into the Desart of *Mardazmay*, where there blew a poisonous Wind, and where the Heat was so vehement, that no Creature could live an Hour in it. Now when the Bears were entered into the Borders of this dangerous Desart, *Maimon*, to engage them farther into it; Come, said he, let us make haste and surprise these accursed Wretches before Day. With such Exhortations he kept them on the March all Night; but the next Day they were astonished to find themselves in so dismal a Place. They not only saw not so much as a Likeness of a Monkey, but they perceived that the Sun had so heated the Air, that the very Birds that flew over the Desart fell down, as it were, roasted to Death; and the Sand was so burning hot, that the Bears Feet were all burned to the Bones. The King, on this, cried out to *Maimon*, Into what a Desart hast thou brought us? And what fierce Whirlwinds are these which I see coming towards us? On this the Monkey, finding they were all too far advanced for the least Possibility of getting back, and therefore sure to perish, spoke boldly; and in Answer to the King of the Bears, Tyrant, said he, know that we are in the Desart of Death; the Whirlwind that approaches us is Death itself, which comes in a Moment to punish thee for all thy Cruelties. And while he was thus speaking, the fiery Whirlwind came and swept them all away.

Two Days after this, the King of the Monkeys returned to his Palace, as *Maimon* foretold him; and finding all his Enemies gone, continued a long Reign in Peace over his Subjects.

Your Majesty, pursued the Vizier, sees by this Example, that there is no trusting to the alluring Words of an Enemy. And, permit me to add, that he ought to perish that seeks the Destruction of others. This Discorse, continued to positively, put the King of the Owls in a Passion, insomuch that he cried to the chief Minister, Why all this Stir to hinder this poor miserable Creature from the Proof of my Clemency? And at the same time commanded his Surgeons to dress *Carchenas*, and to take particular Care of him. You do not consider, added the King, that yourself may one time fall into as great Afflictions as have now befallen him.

Carchenas was now dressed and taken care of by the King's own Surgeon, who soon recovered him from his Wounds. And when he was able to stir about he behaved himself so well, that a little time he won the Love of all the Court. The King of the Owls confided absolutely in him, and began to do nothing without first consulting him. One Day *Charchenas*, addressing himself to the King; Sir, said he, the King of the Ravens has abused me so unjustly, that I shall never die satisfied unless I have first gratified my Revenge. I have been a long time endeavouring to contrive the Means, but find, as the Result of all my Studies about it, that I never can compass it safely nor absolutely, so long as I wear the Shape of a Raven. I have heard, I remember, Persons of Learning and Experience say, that he who has been ill used by a Tyrant, if he makes any Wish by way of Revenge, must, if he would have it succeed, throw himself into the Fire; for that, while he continues there, all his Wishes will be heard. For this Reason I beseech your Majesty that I may be thrown into the Fire, to the end that in the Middle of the Flames I may beg of Heaven to change me into an Owl. Perhaps Heaven will hear my Prayer, and then doubt not, but I shall be able to revenge myself upon my Enemy.

The chief Minister that had always spoken against *Carchenas* was then in the Assembly, and hearing this insinuating Speech. O Traitor, cried he, whither tends all this superfluous Language? Now do I full well know that thou art weaving Mischief, though I cannot divine of what kind it should be; but the Event, I know, will shew it. Sir, added he, turning to the King, caress this wicked Fellow as long as you please, he will never Change his Nature. Does not your Majesty remember that the Mouse was once metamorphosed into a Maid; and yet she could not forbear wishing to have a Rat for her Husband. You love Fables dearly, Vizier, said the King to him, and I will indulge you in your Pleasure, and hear this willingly; but I will not promise you to be a pin the better for it.

FABLE XI.

The MOUSE *that was changed into a* LITTLE GIRL.

A Person of Quality, continued the Vizier, once walking by the Side of a Fountain, saw a very beautiful little Mouse fall at his Feet from the Bill of a Raven who had held it a little too carelessly. The Gentleman, out of Pity, and pleased with its Beauty, took it up, and carried it home; but fearing it should cause Disorder in the Family, as the Women are generally not very fond of these Animals, he prayed to Heaven to change in into a Maid. The Prayer came from the Mouth of a Person of so much Piety and Goodness, that it was heard, and what he requested was presently done; so that, instead of a Mouse, of a sudden he saw before him a very pretty little Girl, whom he afterwards bred up. Some Years after, the good Man seeing his Foster-child big enough to be married, Chuse out, said he to her, in the whole Extent of this Country, the Creature that pleases thee best, and I will make him thy Husband; for I can give thee a Fortune which will make any Body glad to offer his Service to thee. If I may chuse, Sir, for myself in so important an Affair, replied the Maid, let me acknowledge to you, that I am very ambitious. I would, continued she, have a Husband so strong, that he should never be vanquished. That must needs be the Sun, replied the old Gentleman; it is a strange Desire, Child; but, however, thou shalt not want my best Offices in it: And, therefore, the next Morning, said he to the Sun, My Daughter desires an invincible Husband, will you marry her? Alas! answered the Sun, call not me invincible, yonder Cloud enfeebles my Beams; address yourself to that. The good Man, on this, turned and made his Compliment to the Cloud. Alas! said the Cloud, the Wind drives me as it pleases. The old Gentleman, nothing discouraged, desired the Wind to marry his Daughter. But the Wind, laying before him that his Strength was stopped by such a Mountain, he addressed himself to the Mountain. Oh! Sir, said the Mountain, the Rat is stronger than I, for he pierces me in every Side, and eats into my very Bowels; whereupon the old Gentleman, in great Sorrow of Heart, went at length to the Rat, who liked very well the Proposal, and immediately consented to marry his Daughter, saying withal, that he had been a long time seeking out for a Wife. The old Gentleman, on this, returning home, asked his Daughter whether she would be contented to marry a Rat? Now he expected that she should have abhorred the Thoughts of such a Marriage; but was amazed to see her out of Patience to be united to this precious Husband. Thereupon the old Man, with great Sorrow, cried out, Nothing, I find, can alter Nature. In fine, he went to his Prayers again, and desired the Heavens, that they would again turn his Daughter into a Mouse, as she was before; which they accordingly did, and put an end to his Care.

The King of the Owls heard this, and whatever else the Vizier had to say, with great Patience; but attributing all his Remonstrances to his Jealousy of the Raven, took little Notice of them. In the mean time, *Carchenas*, who was all this time a Courtier, and the principal Favourite of the King, had an Opportunity to observe all the Comings and Goings out of the Owls, and whatever else it might be of Service to his Country to know. And when he had perfectly informed himself of every thing, he fairly left them, and returned to the Ravens. On his Arrival in the Raven Camp, he gave the King his Master an Account of every thing that had passed, and said, Now, Sir, is the time for us to be revenged of our Enemies; and what I have seen among them, teaches me how it may be effected. In a certain

Mountain that I know of, and can in a Day's March lead you to, there is a Cave where all the Nation of Owls meet every Day. Now as this Mountain is environed with Wood, your Majesty needs no more but to command your Army to carry a great Quantity of that Wood to the Mouth of the Cave. I will be ready at hand to kindle the Wood, and then let all the Ravens flutter round about to blow the Fire into a Flame. By this Means such Owls as shall adventure out, will be burned in the Flames, and such as stay within shall be smothered; and so shall your Majesty be delivered at once from all your Enemies.

The King highly approved the Raven's Counsel, adored his Courage and Address in his adventurous Enterprize, by which he had learned this; and ordering his whole Army to set forward, they did as *Carchenas* had contrived, and by that Means destroyed at one Instant all the Owls of the Neighbouring Nation.

By this Example we may see, that sometimes Submission to an Enemy is requisite for the eluding of their wicked Designs: Of which the Fable that follows is a yet farther Proof.

F A B L E   XII.

The SERPENT and the FROGS.

A Certain Serpent once became old and feeble, and no longer able to hunt abroad for his Food. In this unfortunate Condition, long he bewailed in Solitude the Infirmities of Age, and wished in vain for the Strength of his youthful Years. Hunger at length, however, taught him, instead of his Lamentations, a Stratagem to get his Livelihood. He went slowly on to the Brink of a Ditch, in the which there lived an infinite Number of Frogs that had just then elected a King to rule over them. Arrived at this Scene of Delight, the wily Serpent seemed to be very sad, and extremely sick; upon which a Frog popped up his Head, and asked him what he ailed? I am ready to starve, answered the Serpent; formerly I lived upon the Creatures of your Species which I was able to take, but now I am so unfortunate, that I cannot catch any thing to subsist on. The Frog, on this Account, went and informed the King of the Serpent's Condition, and his Answer to the Question he asked him. Upon which Report, the King went himself to the Place to look upon the Serpent, who seeing him. Sir, said he, one Day as I was going to snap a Frog by the Foot, he got from me, and fled before me to a certain Dervise's Apartment, and there entered into a dark Chamber, in which there lay a little Infant asleep. At the same time I also entered in pursuit of my Game, and feeling the Child's Foot, which I took for the Frog, I bit it in such a venomous manner, that the Infant immediately died. The Dervise on this, provoked by my Boldness, pursued me with all his Might; but not being able to overtake me, he fell upon his Knees, and begged of Heaven for the Punishment of my Crime, that I might never be able to catch Frogs more, but that I might perish for Hunger, unless their King gave me one or two in Charity; and, lastly, he added to his Wishes, that I might be their Slave and obey them. These Prayers of the Dervise, continued the Serpent, were heard, and I am now come, since it is the Will of Heaven, to submit myself to your Laws, and obey your Orders as long as I live.

The King of the Frogs received his submissive Enemy, with a Acceptance of his Services; but at the same time, it was with great Disdain and swelling Pride that he told him with a haughty Taunt, that he would not disobey the Heavens, but would make use of his Service: And, accordingly, the Serpent got into Employment, and for some Days carried the King upon his Back: But, at length, Most potent Monarch, said he, if you intend that I should serve you long, you must feed me, else I shall starve to death. Thou sayest very true, honest Serpent, replied the King of the Frogs, henceforward I allow thee to swallow two of my Subjects a Day for thy Subsistence. And this was all he had to wish for. Thus the Serpent, by submitting to his Enemy, secured to himself, at his Cost, a comfortable Subsistence during the Remainder of his Life.

To conclude, most sacred Sir, said *Pilpay*, your Majesty sees by these Examples, that Patience is a noble Virtue, and that it greatly conduces to bring about vast Designs. The wife Men of old, Sir, had sufficient Reason to say, that Prudence goes beyond Strength: And your Majesty may see by what I have related, that a Man by his Wit may often redeem himself out of Danger. But your Majesty is also to remember, that these Examples often inform us, that we are never to trust an Enemy, whatever Protestations of Friendship he makes; for in spite of all the fair Speeches of the World, we ought to know that a Raven will be a Raven still. *True Friends* only are, therefore, to be relied upon; and the Conversation and Familiarity of such alone can be truly beneficial to us.